LOVE & HENNESSY 2: AN ADDICTIVE KIND OF LOVE

Carmen Lashay

Text **Treasured** to **444999**
To subscribe to our Mailing List.
Interested in becoming a part of the Treasured Publications family?

Submit manuscripts to
Info@Treasuredpub.com

PROLOGUE
PREVIOUSLY

TOMMIE

It had been a few weeks since I'd seen Landon. Thanksgiving came and left, and I still hadn't seen him. His presence was still felt, though, from the clothes and shoes he had personally delivered to the house with a note attached, saying: *it's getting colder outside, here's some winter clothes since your big ass can't go shopping. And you better not get in your feelings because I called you big. That ass is big.*

He also had lots and lots of stuff delivered for my baby as well. I could tell I was going to have a big problem with him. This baby already had him wrapped around her finger, and she wasn't even born yet. Who buys a baby a custom-made mini Lamborghini power wheel? I guess the same person who would get her six pairs of limited-edition Jordans with the matching jerseys. I just decided to pick and choose my battles with this man, and arguing over his spending and choice of things he bought was a losing battle. I had a better chance of winning the lottery.

Checking my grades for this term after I submitted my final exam, I grabbed a jacket and headed to meet my sister for lunch after I left my therapy session. I was currently at Landon's place because he had kidnapped me. Although he wasn't here now to hold me against my will, he still initially kidnapped me. He complained about not being able to sleep and needing me here for when he went to sleep and woke up. I stayed because I had grown so spoiled and lived for those foot massages and belly rubs. If you'd never been pregnant, then you couldn't possibly understand how amazingly heavenly that feels.

Lying in his bed at night made me feel his presence and helped me sleep better. Since he told me we couldn't be together until I got my confidence back, I started seeing a therapist because I did project a lot of my insecurities onto him, and that wasn't fair to him. Walking outside to the waiting car, I got into the backseat of the car service he'd hired to drive me around. He said I was forbidden from taking an Uber because he didn't trust them, and I didn't need to be pregnant, riding with strangers.

I had my doubts about this supposed car service, though. Not saying they were dangerous; I'm just saying I didn't think they were legit. I thought these were his friends or something, driving me around. I wouldn't speak on it, because I felt safe when I was with them, and it warmed my heart that he really cared enough about me to ensure I was good even when he wasn't around. My only thing was that although he'd done all of this, he hadn't called me, and that had me in my feelings big time.

"Hello, Tommie. How is the little one doing today?" Dr. Phil asked me as I took a seat on his couch. It was crazy that he had the exact same name as the TV show host, and he kind of favored him a bit.

"I'm great, just tired a lot. It's hard work carrying all this weight around. I guess it didn't help that I was already big before this," I said.

"What did we say about that, Tommie? You cannot keep saying things like that."

"I know," I said, twirling my thumbs together.

"What's the real reason for this emergency meeting? Because we are not scheduled to meet again until next week."

"It's Landon. He's been gone almost two weeks, handing an emergency with his business, but he hasn't called me. He's sent gifts, he's sent people to check on me, and he's sent me flowers to the house, but he hasn't called. Does that mean he doesn't like me enough to call?" I cried.

"Tommie, I understand from the little you've told me about your past that you are insecure and have lost all your self-confidence, but you have to stop overthinking things. From what you've told me about Landon, he isn't used to having a girlfriend, so the things he's doing is his way of showing you he likes you. A phone works both ways, and maybe he doesn't want to do all of the work. If you want to talk to him, why not just pick up the phone and shoot him a text or call? You are expecting him to give and give and put himself in a vulnerable state, yet you have nothing to give in return. Try meeting him halfway. This man has told you he likes you and is even more than willing to raise your child with you. A child your ex tried to beat out of you and didn't succeed, yet was successful every other time. Don't push a good man away because you're second guessing his intentions and motives. You are basically not even giving him a chance to mess up on his own because you've already condemned him."

Feeling stupid, I knew everything he said was right. Landon did tell me he liked a confident woman. I was sure he knew I was going crazy, waiting for him to call, but I bet he was just waiting for me to make the first step.

Picking up my phone, I hesitated with pressing two, which was the speed dial number I had installed for him just in case something happened, and I couldn't type his full number. My hands were shaking uncontrollably, and I damn near dropped my phone trying to calm my nerves down. My breathing picked up, and my heartbeat sped up.

"Tommie, I want you to close your eyes and count to five. While you're counting to five, I want you to allow all your insecurities and fears in. Let them in and channel them because once you get to five and open your eyes, I want you to let all of that dissolve and let your confidence soar."

Closing my eyes, I counted out loud.

"One." I thought about all the times I was beaten.

"Two." I thought about the lies and the other women.

"Three." I thought about every miscarriage I had to suffer.

"Four." I thought about all the weight I had gained, which further brought my self-confidence down and caused me to go into major depression.

"Five." I thought about Landon and how he was a good man just trying to show me how a king treats a queen, yet I was pushing him away. Once I got to five, I opened my eyes. My hands had stopped shaking, and I had done exactly what the doc said. I'd dissolved everything to the back of my mind. It wasn't completely gone, but for now, it was at bay. Calling Landon, he answered on damn near the first call.

"Hello, beautiful, how is my daughter doing?" his sexy voice came through the phone.

"Dang, I'm starting to feel left out. That's the only person you want to ask about?" I asked, feigning hurt.

"Naw, but that's the number one leading lady in my life. You're a strong runner up for the second position," he said. This man was like a dream come true the way he loved my baby already. I was also excited that

I could possibly be number two in his life if I got my shit together.

"What have you been up to?" he asked me.

"Missing you," I boldly stated.

"Really? Is that right?" he asked, I guess caught off guard by my answer.

"Yes, I miss you rubbing my belly and my feet. They hurt something terrible now," I said.

"Using me for my skills; that's fucked up, ma," he laughed. "I thought you was gon' say you miss this fire ass head I threw on you. Hell, I thought you was in a coma when you was just staring up at the ceiling," he said then shocked me even further when he started singing Tank. It didn't shock me that he knew the song. What shocked me was the fact he could actually sing. "Them young boys didn't know what to do with it. You got it all in my face. I like the way that it taste. When you got it all on my plate, it won't go to waste. That's what you get every day when you fucking with me."

My panties were soaked at this point, and my breathing was erratic. I had to calm myself down because, for a second, I forgot I was still in the doctor's office.

"Ain't that what you was listening to that day in the kitchen, ma? You gon' let a nigga taste it again?

Because I feel like I'm addicted now. Shit tastes good as fuck. I be having to try my best lying beside you not to taste that shit because of your first reaction, but now, I need another dose," he said.

I nodded my head like an idiot as if he could actually see me.

"Yes," I said barely above a whisper.

"Good, because I'm eating that shit all night long when I get back. But listen, baby, daddy's gotta go. I'll call you back later," he said before he hung up.

I closed my eyes for a few seconds to gather myself together. Then, I opened them and stared at my therapist with my face flushed.

"I take it that conversation went well," he said, smiling as if he knew exactly what we were talking about.

"Thank you," was all I choked out before I hurriedly left out of the office. When I got outside, as always, the car was still waiting for me.

Ring, ring!

"Hello?"

"Tommie, your mom is in the hospital. It's not looking too good. I figured you would want to know and be here," Amber said in a rushed voice. We had slowly gotten back on the right track after she forgave me for leaving and not telling her.

"Oh my God," I yelled, feeling as if time had stopped. "I'm on my way."

Quickly hanging up, I called Jasmine.

"Bitch, you're running late," she said when she answered.

"Jas," I cried out.

"What's wrong, Tommie? Is it the baby? Where are you?" she screamed.

"My mom is in the hospital, and it's looking bad," I cried.

"Okay, I'm booking your flight now. Come to my house, and let's call your physician to see if you are cleared to fly even though you're barely seven months."

"Okay," I said, telling the driver to take me to Jas's house. I never had to give him directions, because he always seemed to know where everything in my life was at, down to my father's house, whom I had been spending a lot of more time with lately. I called Landon back, but he didn't answer, so I left him a voice message, telling him what happened and that I was going home to check on my mom. A couple hours later, I found myself back in a place I never thought I would return.

Waddling into the hospital with Jas on my side and my driver behind us, who I was starting to think wasn't a driver at all, we all headed to my mother's room. Amber had told me what room they were in and promised to wait there until I arrived. Pushing the door open, the sight before me caused me to drop to my knees.

"Mommy," I cried out as everyone, doctors included, tried helping me up.

"Tommie, you have to be strong for her," Jas said, rubbing my hair as everyone helped me to a chair.

"This is the daughter? Hi, I'm Dr. Lopez, your mother's doctor."

Nodding my head at him, he continued. "Her body is under a lot of stress, and she hasn't been taking her medicine like she's supposed to. She is in stage three breast cancer, and right now, we need to aggressively attack the cancer cells and operate immediately, or we don't predict she'll make it past the month," he told me.

I had to blink a few times to make sure this wasn't a dream. Just a few hours ago, I was happy and content with life, and now, my mother was in a coma and dying. In all the emails that we'd exchanged, she never once mentioned it. Now, not only would my baby not have a biological father, but she would never see her grandmother either. This was enough to drive anyone crazy, and I felt like I was about to pass out. I couldn't take this.

"Noooo," I cried as everything faded black.

Beep, beep, beep.

Opening my eyes, I looked around and noticed I was in a hospital bed. My eyes landed on Jasmine balled up in a chair, texting.

"What happened?"

"Thank God you're awake," she said, coming over to my bed. "You scared the shit out of me. Your blood pressure spiked too high, causing you to pass out. You have to calm down, sis. I know it's hard, but you're already high-risk due to your high blood pressure. Think about Royalty. I know it's hard, but you have to just relax."

"Can you take me to see my mom?" I asked her. I heard everything she'd said, and I would never intentionally put my baby at risk. I was going to try and calm down.

"First, we are going to go get you changed up, let you shower, and get some food in your system. Then, you can come back and see your mother, and don't even think of debating me on this, or I will call Ghost," she threatened me.

My own sister would willingly snitch on me to that psycho who already thought this was his baby. I did not want those problems, so I just nodded my head and cooperated because I knew Ghost would flip out if he assumed I was doing something to harm his baby. Going to our hotel, we ordered room service, and I went to take a shower. The water felt so good on my body that I spent almost an hour in there. Once I came out, I dried off and threw on a sundress and started eating my food. Jasmine came into my room, because we had a two-bedroom suite, and handed me a pill.

"Here, take this. It will regulate your blood pressure until we can get your prescription filled. The perks of dating a doctor."

"I thought you were dating Dom?"

"Girl, me and the entire tri state area."

"Well, was the sex even worth the wait?" I asked. Hell, I was curious only because Dom had more females than a football field had yards.

"Sex? Girl I don't know what you're talking about," she said.

"Play slow," I said.

"Okay, I'll tell you if you tell me what the hell you and Ghost was doing the night I told you not to wait up for me. I came home to you screaming like you were being murdered, talking about *eat it, daddy*," she said. I damn near choked on the sandwich I was eating.

"We wasn't doing anything," I said as my face turned beet red.

"Whelp, me and Dom did the same thing—not anything that is."

"Touché, hoe, touché," I said because I didn't even have a valid comeback for that one. Hearing my phone ringing, I searched for it to answer it.

"Hello," I said once I finally found it.

"Tommie, your cousins and nem at my house, and I kinda accidentally told everybody you was home, so now, they're all waiting to see you before everybody heads up to the house," Amber said. I couldn't even be mad at her, because I owed my entire family an explanation for my disappearance. Working with Dr. Phil taught me to embrace my past and not be ashamed of it, so I was going to get it all out—the abuse and lies. I was done living a lie, pretending like I was somebody that people should be jealous of.

That was the problem with people. They kept up a lie so long that they started to believe it themselves. People saw me and saw the money, cars, and clothes, and immediately envied me. They didn't know I was getting cheated on left and right, depressed, and getting my ass beat every other night. Never judge a book by its cover, because their cover might be nice, and you might call that 'relationship goals,' but the story in that book could be fucked up.

"Okay, I'll be over there soon. Tell everyone I love them."

"That was your best friend?" Jasmine asked with a roll of her eyes.

"Yeah, and why you don't like Amber?"

"Because it's something about her that is so fake to me, but that's your bestie, so if you're rocking with her, then I am too," she said, grabbing her purse.

"You're the best big sister a girl could ever have," my emotional ass said.

"You better know it," she replied, leaving out the room. Finishing my sandwich up, I grabbed my purse, room key, and phone and headed to the living room where Jasmine was smiling in Mark's face.

"You wanna meet me at the hospital, huh?" I asked her with a smirk.

"Actually, Mark was just leaving. He is the one who brought you the medicine," she said with a devilish look on her face, letting me know that wasn't the only thing he brought.

"Nice seeing you again, Tommie. I see you've progressed rather well in your pregnancy. That little lady is a fighter for sure. You're glowing, and pregnancy suits you very well," he said.

"Thank you, Dr. Mark, and nice seeing you again as well," I said.

We decided to leave out with him, and after he made sure we were safely in the car and walked off, I said, "What else did he drop off besides medicine?"

"Nothing, I can't believe what you are insinuating," Jasmine said with her hand over her chest like she was appalled. Laughing at her, I told our driver the address that we were going and sat back in my seat, anxious to see my family. Pulling up and getting out of the car, I walked up to her apartment, took a breath and knocked on the door. When it opened, I barely had time to react before I was attacked.

"Tommie," my family shouted, practically jumping on me.

"Here I was, thinking something happened to your ass, but the whole time, you were out getting dicked down. I see why you ain't have time to call us," one of my twin cousins said to me.

"Girl, you've been cheating on Rodney?" Chelsea asked. "I guess that explains why I saw him with a new girlfriend. She's not bad looking," she just had to toss out.

"This is very much Rodney's baby," I said, rolling my eyes at her because this bitch was really testing me. I wouldn't be surprised if she had been fucking him as much shade as she tossed at me whenever she was around.

"My bad. I wasn't trying to say it wasn't. I was just saying we were all thrown for a loop when he started flossing her around town, and she was even driving your truck," she felt the need to add.

"Yeah, I was two seconds from beating the bitch up, but Rodney told everybody you left him for another nigga," my cousin said. I looked around, and everybody was looking at me, waiting for me to clear up a few things. I guess everybody thought I skipped town with some made-up ass nigga because I surely didn't know where I found said nigga.

"Look, I know you guys are concerned, but my sister doesn't need everybody coming at her at once. That's not good for my niece. She will, however, answer anything she feels like answering right now, and the rest, shit, y'all will have to fill in the gaps yourself," Jasmine spoke up.

"Well, it's okay if you got dumped, boo. It happens. You just don't take off," Chelsea again said.

That was it.

"Look, bitch, all this shade you keep throwing is about to get your ass beat—pregnant or not. Just get it off your chest and stop beating around the bush! You're fucking Rodney and prolly been fucking him, and you want me to know. Newsflash, hoe, I don't give a fuck."

"Girl, ain't nobody fucking that nigga that you *thought* was yours, but newsflash, everybody and they momma knew that nigga was for everybody."

Whap!

Jasmine had reached around me and punched her ass dead in her mouth.

"Don't let the title 'doctor' fool you, bitch. I can get down with the best of them. You got me all the way fucked up, thinking you gon' come for that one," Jasmine said.

"Yeah, Chelsea, that shit ain't fucking cool. You see our cousin's pregnant, and yo' hoe ass wanna talk shit to her. Bitch, we'll beat your ass," the twins said.

Laughing, she said, "It's funny how y'all really think I'm the one that's the threat or broke up her happy home."

"Everybody, calm down," Amber jumped in saying.

"Fuck this. I'm out of here. I don't have time for this shit. Let's go, Jasmine," I said, opening the door just as a car pulled up.

"Daddy," Karter said from behind me. I didn't even notice him in the house, and I felt bad that all the commotion happened around him.

"Tommie, there is my daddy," he said excitedly. At least something good was coming from this visit because I had never met his father. The driver side door opened, and I got the shock of my life, watching Ghost get out, followed by Rodney from the passenger side.

CHAPTER 1

GHOST

Sitting in my car in Houston, Texas, watching the traffic flowing in and out of Henry's folks house, I couldn't wrap my head around the fact that something wasn't right. I always went with my gut, and my gut was telling me that it was more to this story than what I was told. This was why I reached out to Kelina to do some additional digging for me. Kelina was my on-again, off-again fling; I wouldn't call her a girlfriend.

Aside from always getting my dick right and being bad as fuck, she was a beast with locating information and tracking down a muthafucka who thought they could disappear. You would never know she was so geeky because she was fine as fuck. Picking up my phone, I dialed her number because I needed that information ASAP. I was ready to get back home to Tommie. Shit, I had already missed Thanksgiving; I wasn't trying to be up here longer than I needed to be. The only reason I hadn't run up in that house yet was because I didn't exactly know what I would be walking into since she specifically said my name. That and the fact that there were people always here, and I even saw a few detectives and cops coming and going. I wasn't sure what all this nigga was into, but it cost zilch to be prepared.

"Hey," she said casually, answering the phone like this was a damn social call.

"Cut to the chase, Kelina. What you got for me?"

"So that's what we've been reduced to? No *hey, baby girl. How you doing? What's been up, sexy?*"

"You know what? Fuck it, I'll find somebody else to get the information for me," I said, prepared to hang up.

"Henry was an undercover federal agent. The information you pulled was accurate, except the part that Henry had been deep undercover for years as a mule—first under your father, and now under you. It says he has a partner, but no name was listed for him," she said all in one breath.

“Shit. You not bullshitting me, huh?”

“No, I wouldn’t make some shit like this up,” she said.

“Good looking out,” I said as I hung up. I was thankful for the fact that I liked to think before I reacted because had I just run up in that house and laid everybody down, my black ass would be tried, convicted, and sentenced in less than thirty seconds. Starting up the car, I got my ass out of there, and decided first thing in the morning, I was shutting down my entire operation for a week.

This was why I never did shit where I slept; so none of my businesses could be tied back to the drug shit, and nobody even knew my full information. I was Ghost to these niggas—nothing more, nothing less. A few days was all everybody got off because I had no plans of losing a lot of money over this bullshit. Hell, I had mouths to feed with a whole crew counting on me, so I planned to reopen and have everything moved around, including drop days and trap houses.

Thankfully, Henry was only a mule, and mules weren’t privy to much information, but his partner might be deeper than him. To my knowledge, they had already killed Johnny’s ass, so he couldn’t be the mole. I didn’t have the slightest clue who the fucking mole was, but I was gon' work overtime to feed his ass false information since they would be trying to close the case and bring me in now that Henry was dead.

The question, though, was, if I left him alone, why would he think I was going to kill him and tell his mom that if he died, I did it? I should have just killed his ass that day, and I wouldn't be having this fucking problem. No witnesses, and shoot to kill had always been my motto. Once you started saving people, this was the shit that would come back to bite you in the ass.

Driving myself straight to the airport, I pressed a button on my keys, detonating a bomb that I had stashed at the apartment I had rented out under an alias name. I didn't need anything being traced back to me. After I made it to the airport and was halfway to my destination, I had plans of blowing up this car as well. It would save me from having to extra scrub everything down. It was guaranteed they wouldn't find one damn traceable print from this C4. It was a risk sleeping and driving a car with explosives, but that just proved a nigga wasn't scared to die. Shit, we lived in a world where death was forever present anyway, so it made no difference to me.

Back at home, I walked around, looking for Tommie, and noticed her suitcase was missing. Calling her phone, I didn't get an answer, so I called Jasmine.

"You on your way?" she asked as soon as she answered.

"On my way where?"

"Shit, Ghost, I didn't even look at the number; I just answered the phone."

"Okay, where's Tommie?"

"She's currently in the hospital, but they are releasing her tomorrow. They're only keeping her tonight because her blood pressure shot up, and she passed out."

"What the fuck!" I yelled, jumping up from the spot I had just laid down in.

"What hospital? I'm on my way," I said, jumping up, grabbing my keys.

"We are at a hospital in Atlanta. I'm sending you the name and address."

Grabbing the bridge of my nose and pinching it, I mentally counted down from ten to control my anger because I felt myself about to fucking go off. Here I was, coming home from a long few weeks of work, looking for my girl, and she was in an entirely different state that nobody fucking bothered to inform me about, and not only that, but she was in the hospital.

"Jasmine, what are y'all doing in Atlanta?"

"She left you a voice message. Her mom has cancer and collapsed. She is in a coma, and it's not looking too good. She's in the third stage, and they need to attack it aggressively now, or she won't survive the month. They told Tommie this information, and she broke down crying and passed out. Tomorrow, I plan to find a room for us to check into, make sure she eats, and then, we'll come back up here to see her mom. Being that my on-again, off-again boyfriend works here, I'll get all the information on her mother and tell her myself so she won't have another spell," she said.

Atlanta? Small world. I never even bothered to ask her where she was running away from. Come to think of it, I didn't even know her ex nigga's name.

"Okay, listen, I'm booking the next flight out of here, and I'll have my cousin pick me up from the airport. Book a nice hotel, and put it on my credit card—the one I gave you in case of emergencies. Make sure it's a double-room suite so we can kill two birds with one stone, and I won't be driving around looking for one," I said, not giving her a chance to reply before I hung up. I had one more call to make.

"Yo, ugly ass nigga, about time you rejoined the little people," Dom said.

"Nigga, yo' wide back ass has never been little, but listen up because I got some important shit to tell you. I have to go to Atlanta for a few days, so I really need you to handle this shit for me."

"Damn, ole traveling ass nigga, I took one vacation to see Moms, and yo' ass took that as you could be gone months at a time."

"Man, not right now, D. This is serious. Henry's a fed. I need you to shut everything down for a week. During that week, move everything around, switch everything up, and everybody gets a new drop date and location. Clear out all the traps and have a few of your hoes come scrub the warehouse from top to bottom. I don't plan on being gone but a week, so when I get back, I'll open everything back up just in different locations, and getting the information gon' be on a need-to-know basis."

"Damn, man, this shit just blew my high. How the fuck did we miss that one?"

"Shit, it's a lot I got to fill you in on, on that topic, but now, I have to go see about my girl. She's in the hospital."

"Damn, sis okay?"

"Man, I don't even know. I'll keep you in the loop. One love."

Hopping on the internet, I went to Expedia and booked a one-way ticket to Atlanta, GA. I didn't know the exact day I was leaving, but I planned to be out of there and back to business as soon as possible. Since my plane didn't leave until 3:00 a.m., I busied myself with packing and getting everything together and in order.

I also sat down and went over the books from my businesses and checked the bank logs, monitoring the accounts, making sure the amount dropped off matched the amount from the log that day sent over by the manager from each business. I was a thorough ass nigga and always made time to make sure my money was straight, and a nigga wasn't skimming thousands of dollars off my shit. After I finished, I went to take a nap so that I could hit the ground running when I got in town.

"Good looking on picking me up," I said to my cousin as we got into the car.

"Shit, why you just ain't rent a car?" he asked.

“Because I have a car. I just needed a ride to it,” I told him matter-of-factly. I had purchased a car when I decided I would come down for Christmas because I didn’t want to go through the hassle of renting and returning.

“Well cool, we’ll go get your car; then, you can follow me to drop my car off, and I’ll hop in the car with you because I haven’t seen you in a minute, so I’m rolling with you, bro,” he said. That was fine by me. I told him where the dealership was. When we got there, however, they were still closed.

“Shit, they open in almost an hour, let’s go get some food then come back,” he said. As if right on cue, my stomach started growling.

“Shit, a nigga is hungry, so we can do that, but let’s not go too far. I need to get this car and go see about my baby,” I said.

“Nigga, since I picked you up, yo’ sprung ass been talking about this girl. I gotta meet this bitch who locked you down,” he laughed. Even though I knew he was just joking, I still felt some type of way about him calling Tommie a bitch.

“Aye, watch that word in reference to my girl.”

“My bad,” he said, throwing his hands up in surrender. Laughing at his crazy ass, I sat back and enjoyed the feeling of being home as we headed to get food. Thirty minutes later, we found ourselves back in the car after stopping at McDonald’s for breakfast. As we pulled off and headed back to the dealership, I pulled out my phone to check my messages. I had hit Jasmine up earlier, but I’m guessing she was still sleep. I had a few messages, but the only one of importance to me was the one from Jasmine telling me they had left the hospital, went to the hotel to get dressed, and were on the way back to the hospital, and now they’d stopped by Amber’s place.

“Her ass just can’t be still,” I mumbled.

“What?”

“Naw, man, my sister texted me, telling me my girl left the hospital and is at her friend’s place. Her ass gon’ make me break my foot off in her ass. She got big and pregnant with my baby and doing all these extra activities,” I said, frustrated because I didn’t want her going anywhere else without me. Especially not somewhere where she might run into the fuck nigga she called her ex. If he even tried to touch her, I knew I was killing his ass.

"Momma gon' be super happy your light-skinned ass is home. She's really been missing you," he said.

"Yeah, I've been missing her crazy, old ass as well. How the diabetes been since she beat it? Has it flared back up?"

"Naw, bruh, she's good, back moving around, and very active. Hell, her ass be in everybody's shit. She needs a damn grandbaby to keep her occupied and out my relationship," he said, laughing. "I can't wait to tell her you got a baby on the way. Watch her try and move up there and get on your nerves."

"Shit, she's more than welcome to," I said because that didn't sound like a bad idea. Tommie would need as much help as she could get when the baby was born. We pulled up to the car lot, and I was in and out in under twenty minutes, which I was thankful for. After I jumped into my car, I followed Rodney to drop his car off and even met his new woman, who happened to be the chick he hooked up with when he came to Jersey.

"So I see y'all still going strong," I said as soon as he hopped into my car.

"Hell yeah. I had to cancel my last bitch to get my mind right."

Shaking my head, I said, "Nigga, you're stupid, but you should have kept the one who was down when you ain't have shit. Them be the most loyal ones."

"Shit, you would think that, but these hoes not loyal, and nigga got picture evidence, proving her fat ass was outchea doing the most."

"Damn," I said, making a right and heading down a street, searching for the house Jasmine sent me the address to. I was now driving, and we were headed to the address to where they were.

"Who stays this way? You know?"

"My sister and girl over here with her friend. She ain't seen everybody in a while, so shit, they're catching up."

"Man, I know the hoe that live here. That ain't nobody friend. Bitch still trying to pin a baby on me, but I know the little nigga ain't mine. That pussy super friendly," he said. "I do send money here and there for the kid, and I been meaning to get a blood test."

"Damn, how old is he?" I asked because that shit sounded crazy. Hoes were scandalous like that, though. I pulled into the driveway and was getting out when he continued talking as he also opened his door to get out.

"Daddy!" I heard a voice say. Looking up, I saw Tommie standing in the doorway, looking like she'd seen a ghost. It literally looked like all the color had drained from her face. As the little boy ran past me to Rodney, I continued walking toward her. Taking her into my arms, I hugged her tightly because I missed her. When she didn't hug me back, I pulled back, and before I could ask her what was up, Rodney cut me off.

"What the fuck, Ghost? How you know my bitch?" Turning to Tommie, he said, "So that's what we're doing? We're keeping it all in the family? Bruh, please don't tell me this who you been tellin' me about," he said, pointing at Tommie, laughing hysterically.

Looking her dead in the eyes, I said, "So you've been fucking my cousin and trying to play me like a sucker?"

"No-no, I haven't been fucking him. Well, not since I ran away from him. He is my ex-boyfriend, Royalty's father, and the man who damn near beat me to death," she cried. Hearing her say this, I became so damn enraged. Here this was, the woman I wanted to build a life with, and she turned out to be my cousin's baby momma. This shit could not be happening to me. Just when I thought I had found the one, I committed the ultimate betrayal by going against the code.

Still, it didn't sit right with me that this was the nigga who damn near killed my daughter. Come to think of it, he damn near killed them both and left them for dead, fucked hoes every time he came home, and was just telling me about these twins he fucked yesterday, so fuck him and his feelings. I knew this would change our relationship; I just hoped he wasn't dumb enough to fuck with the business aspect of it because, blood or not, anybody could get laid down about my money.

"Let's go," I said, grabbing her by her arms.

"So you really leaving with this bitch, cuz? This fat bitch fucked my cousin then got him playing Daddy to that bastard," was the last word I let him get out before I pushed Tommie out of the way and dove on his ass.

"Nigga, I don't give a fuck what you got going on; you gon' watch your fucking mouth when you speaking on my girl and especially my fucking seed. Cousin or no cousin, you know how I give it up, so fuck with me, Rodney!" I yelled between each punch, getting madder by the minute because all this shit had my head spinning. My cousin, my brother, the nigga I actually trusted with my life, shit, the only family a nigga really had, and I was beating his ass like a nigga in the streets, over somebody that was his baby momma. This shit was just crazy.

CHAPTER 2

TOMMIE

I was too busy trying to process everything that was going on to even stop and realize that Ghost had walked up to me, and Karter ran past him to Rodney. Turning to look at my best friend, my sister, someone whom I loved dearly, reality set in, and I ran and slapped the shit out of her. “You bitch!” I yelled.

Hearing all the commotion, my sister, cousins, and Chelsea all ran outside to see what was going on. I guess Amber called herself trying to hit me back, but my sister caught her ass in mid swing and did some type of damn move that resulted in Amber being put on her ass in two-point-five seconds.

Where the fuck did she learn that from? I paused to think to myself.

"I wish the fuck you would, bitch!" Jasmine yelled down to her as she looked up at me in confusion. Looking past me, she finally noticed Ghost and Rodney.

"What the fuck is going on around here?" she yelled, running over to them, trying break them apart. At this point, Ghost had Rodney in a chokehold, trying to put his ass to sleep. I watched as Karter was kicking Ghost in the leg, trying to get him off of his daddy. Being that he was my godson, and I loved him dearly, I wasn't even thinking clearly right now, because if I was, I would have made making sure he was safe my number one priority. However, I felt that I was off my rocker, so I turned back to Amber. Seeing this as my opportunity, I ran back over to her ass and, as best as I could, reached back and punched her dead in the face. She hopped up quick, and we started going blow for blow until my cousins jumped in and started beating her ass, which I was glad for because I was out of breath, my back hurt, and I could barely stand up, but I didn't care about any of that at this point. I felt hurt and betrayed, and somebody was gon' feel me.

"I don't know what the fuck is going on, and I don't give a damn, but bitch, you just not about to fucking hit my cousin while she big and pregnant!"

Kenyatta yelled, grabbing Amber by her long weave and punching her.

"Hell naw! Bitch got us fucked up," Kenya, her twin sister, said, getting some licks in. Mad and all, I could admit Amber wasn't backing down even though they were both giving her ass the ass whooping her mother should have given her.

"Y'all wrong as fuck for jumping that girl!" Chelsea yelled from behind me. Quickly spinning around, I went to hit her ass, but before I could, I felt myself being lifted off my feet and into the air.

"That's enough!" Ghost yelled so loudly that even the twins stopped fighting and looked at him as if to say they didn't want no problems at all. Heaving up and down, he put me down just as Amber felt that was the perfect time to run up on me and hit me. Before I could react about the fact this nigga was holding me, shit hit me. All I heard was "dammmmn" and looked down to see her back on her ass. It took me a minute to process the fact that Ghost had knocked her ass out. I wasn't sure if he'd punched her, slapped her, or what, but the shit sounded off.

"I want you to try that shit again, bitch, and I'll break your fucking jaw!" he barked. I felt bad for how hard he had hit her and was slightly mad for a split second, but then, I remembered she was the snake ass bitch fucking my nigga, and my godson was really my stepson.

"Mommy," I heard Karter say as he ran to her with tears running down his face.

"Somebody get the baby," I was saying as Ghost practically dragged me to the car.

"I'm not fucking leaving without my sister!" I yelled as Ghost opened the car door and put me inside.

"Sit your pregnant as the fuck down and don't move!" he yelled at me before slamming the door so hard I was surprised it didn't break. I watched as he walked over to Jasmine and the twins as Chelsea struggled to pick Amber up off the ground. Rodney walked up to them, saying something that I couldn't make out to Ghost. Thinking he would start fighting Ghost again because of him hitting Amber, that wasn't the case. It seemed like only words were exchanged as he grabbed Karter and walked off down the street, pulling out his phone to call someone but pausing to give me a death stare before continuing on his way. A few minutes later, our driver pulled up, and Jas got in the car with him, and they pulled off. The twins then came over to the car and opened my door.

"You okay, Tommie?" they both asked at the same time, something they hated doing but always seemed to do.

"Yeah, I'm fine," I said even though my breathing was coming in strained still.

"It's on sight for that hoe every time we see her. I can't believe she did that shit. I never even looked at Karter enough to notice the resemblance," Kenyatta said. As soon as they saw Ghost walking up, they both quickly hugged me and walked to their car, but not before making me promise to keep in touch. I agreed and closed my door. As soon as Ghost got in the car, I started going off.

"Where that bitch ass nigga going with my godson? Why you let the nigga walk away? And what the fuck y'all got to talk about?" I yelled, my mind racing a mile a minute as I fired off every question as it popped in my brain. I was slowly losing it, and didn't know what to think or do. My newfound love interest and my old love interest were related. Cousins. Ain't this about a bitch.

"Shut the fuck up, Tommie. You're really trying a nigga right now."

"You act like I'm the one in the fucking wrong!"

"You are. You're already high risk, yet yo' ass out here fucking fighting and shit and over another nigga like you still got feelings for him or something!" he barked as he started the car and pulled off. "My fucking seed better be okay."

"That bitch fucked my nigga then smiled in my face for years, but I'm in the wrong?"

"Your nigga, huh? That's how you feel?"

"You know what the fuck I meant!" I said, waving him off as I rubbed my stomach because Royalty had started cutting up. Her little ass was kicking me like she was mad Ghost and I were fighting or some shit.

"Naw, I don't know shit, so how about you let me fucking know because you're starting to look real suspect right about now. You was with him for as long as you was, and you're telling me you never knew shit about me? Help me understand, ma, because my pictures all up and through his mom's house, so let a real nigga know what's good," he said, pulling up to the hospital and cutting the engine.

"What you mean?"

"Shit, I just beat the fuck out my damn brother, shit! Fuck cousin; we're more like brothers, and I fought that nigga like a regular nigga on the street. I've known him my entire life; I just met you. I need to know that you not on some damn bullshit ass 'get back' games with that nigga, and you specifically targeted me."

"You sound stupid as fuck. If that was the case, I wouldn't have fucking worked for you even on days I didn't feel like it. I would have just hopped on your dick and got to the money. That's getting back at a nigga, but the most you have done is tasted the pussy, so miss me with that bullshit," I said, struggling to get out the car, slamming the door, and wobbling toward the entrance.

I didn't even know where that person that I seemed to transform into back there came from, but I did know I liked her and planned on keeping her around because I was tired of people thinking they could say anything they wanted to me and I just had to take it. Fuck that. I was fed the fuck up. It was only so far you could push a person before they decided to push back. I could hear Ghost behind me as I opened the door and walked inside. I was headed toward the elevators when he stopped me.

"Where you going?"

"To see my mom."

"Later," he said, pulling me toward the front desk and checking me in.

"What you mean, later? And why you checking me into the hospital? I'm fine."

"You're not fine. You may think I don't pay attention, but I know and observe everything that goes on with you like the fact you been rubbing your stomach and back since you got in the car, or the fact that you can barely get your breathing under control. You're checking on my seed first. Jasmine's doctor friend already gave us the information on what room your mom's in and the fact she is resting, so you can wait a little while," he said with authority. Rolling my eyes at him, I snatched away and went to sit down, pushing his hands away from me when he attempted to help me in the chair.

"Stop being so fucking stubborn and let a nigga help you. Damn, you're beginning to piss me the fuck off."

"What you gon' do? Beat my ass like Rodney used to?" I asked but immediately regretted. "I didn't mean that," I said as his jaw clenched, and he went away from me. Tears came to my eyes as I watched him walk out the door. I was an emotional wreck right now, and all I wanted to do besides see my mother was leave and go home. I needed my bed and my therapist. 'Bout time Ghost walked back over to me, the doctor was calling my name to come to the back. Without saying a word to me, he left me to struggle to get up as I wobbled behind him and the doctor.

"So what brings you in today, Ms. Knowles?" the doctor asked, looking down at the charts.

"I had an altercation with an old friend, and now, my back hurts, and my breathing is irregular," I said, rubbing my stomach in a circular motion. Writing on his chart, the doctor replied, "When you say altercation, what exactly are you referring to?"

Putting my head down in shame as the reality of me being six months and pregnant hit me, I was now embarrassed to admit it out loud.

"She got into a fight, doc, so now, we just want to make sure her and the baby are okay," Ghost spoke up and said.

"Ohhh," the doctor replied. "Well, we can definitely check on you both to see if you didn't create any problems for you guys. I can't stress enough how very dangerous that was because anything could happen to you or your child. Getting hit the wrong way could result in brain damage or any other very serious problems. You could even put your child in risk of losing their life all because of a decision you chose to make."

"I know, and I take full responsibility for my actions. I just want to make sure my baby girl is okay, and if she is, I promise I will never put her life in danger again," I said as tears fell down my eyes. I hated how my emotions were all over the place right now. After doing a very thorough check up on me, the doctor prescribed me some medicine for my back pains and gave me strict orders to stay off my feet. Leaving out of the room, I pulled my phone out and sent my sister a text, seeing if she was okay and where she was.

Waiting for her to respond, I walked toward the elevator, pressing for it to come down. Ghost ignored me the entire time and had barely said two words to me. He did, however, have tons of questions for the doctor. I didn't care on one hand, but on the other, I did. I felt bad about the comment I'd made to him, but at the same time, I was still very much angry with the whole situation, and the fact remained that he was related to and raised with the person who brought me so much pain.

I didn't know where the status of our relationship stood, but for right now, it was nonexistent. My feelings for him got turned off like a water faucet the minute he got out of the car with Rodney's ass. It was crazy that I loved two cousins. This was truly some Maury, Jerry

Springer type shit. Walking to my mother's room, I exhaled deeply, trying to get myself together before I went inside. Feeling Ghost place his hands on my shoulder, I wanted nothing more than to fall in his arms and let him hold me and reassure me that everything was going to be okay. I wanted my best friend back, but my wall was slowly coming back up as I shrugged him off and turned the knob, going inside the room. Seeing my mom with tubes, my knees almost gave out.

"Here. Sit down, ma," Ghost said from behind me. Feeling too weak to fight with him, I let him guide me to a chair to sit down. My heart literally broke seeing my mother like this. I felt the same way I did the first time I saw her. I thought since I had seen her once already, it would be easier this go around, but it wasn't easier at all.

"Listen, if you can't calm down, I'm taking you back to the hotel room, and you gon' be banned from coming up here."

"You can't do that," I said in between crying.

"Try me, Tommie," he said, calling me by my full name, so I knew he meant business. Not wanting to be stopped from coming to see my mother, I tried desperately to get myself together.

"Let me go find a doctor and speak to them separately. I don't need you hearing anything. From now on, not even Jasmine can tell you anything. If you need to know something, I'll tell you. You've already passed out once, and you're high risk. I'm not putting my child's life in danger, and before you say some stupid shit to piss me off, yes, that's still my fucking seed, and I'll kill any fucking body who tries to tell me differently," he said as he walked out the door in search of a doctor.

I didn't know how I felt about him being adamant about still wanting to be in my child's life. I wasn't sure whether I was overjoyed or upset. I just wished I could restart this day because this wasn't how I envisioned it going when I opened my eyes earlier. Walking over to my mom's bed, I pulled a chair up close, sat down, grabbed her hand, and laid my head down. I was mentally, physically, and emotionally exhausted. Before I knew it, I had closed my eyes and drifted off to sleep.

CHAPTER 3

GHOST

When I returned to the room after talking to the doctors, I found Tommie knocked out. Picking her up effortlessly, like she wasn't six months pregnant, I carried her to the elevator and out to the car. Making sure she was safely tucked away in bed at the hotel, I left back out to go get her prescription filled. Once I returned to the room, I saw that she was still sleeping peacefully.

I still couldn't get over the fact that she really came out her mouth and said was I going to beat her like Rodney did. That shit fucked me up inside, and for that reason, I doubted I could ever fuck with her like that again. I'd always communicate with her for the sake of my child, but for her to accuse me of something so vile, I just didn't see myself ever coming back from that.

Stretching, I went to take a shower and chill. I left out of the room and made myself a drink then came back and went into the bathroom. Thirty minutes later, I emerged, feeling refreshed and rejuvenated.

Knock, knock!

I already knew it was Jasmine since she had the adjoining room, so I walked over to the door and opened it. Walking in, she looked at the bed, noticing Tommie asleep, so I followed her back outside into the living room.

"How is she?"

"Besides a fucked-up individual that needs serious help, she's good."

"Damn, that's harsh. I know you're mad about the fight, but I mean, that was her supposed best friend and her boyfriend who she was with for years. Granted, I'd been knew the bitch was a snake the first day I met her, but this is Tommie we're talking about. She likes to see the good in everybody."

"Yeah, well, that's all fine and dandy, but I'm not fucking with her if it isn't about my child. You know today, during an argument, she let some dumb shit fly out her mouth like *oh, you gon' beat my ass like Rodney did.*"

By the way Jasmine eyes expanded, it was clear she was just as shocked as I was.

"I- I. Well, she, she umm…"

"Save it," I told her, holding my hand up, signaling for her to stop any lie she had on the tip of her tongue to say. "You know that's not even in me to put my hands on a female. I'll rough one up, or choke their ass up, but actually beat they ass like a nigga is some shit I would never do. Hoes like her friend Amber are the exception to the rule, but I wouldn't beat her ass, though. She ain't exempt from catching a bullet, though."

"That bitch had it coming, so fuck her. You should have beat her ass senseless. It's on sight every time I see that hoe. Some hoes just need to be beat."

"Calm down, Mike Tyson, and true, but that's beside the point I'm trying to make, and the fact that Tommie would even let that come out of her mouth blows me. We were making good progress, and now this," I said, shaking my head, taking another gulp of my drink.

"I know she didn't mean it. Just give her time."

"She can have all the time she needs because a nigga's not fucking with her like that no more. You know me. I'm a no-tolerance type of nigga. You got one time to fuck up with me," I said to her. I didn't know why sis was trying so hard, because she knew me better than most, so she knew that I was done. "Fuck all that, though. Let's talk about you. It's been awhile since we had a sit down, and it's apparently much needed."

"What you talking about?"

"The fact that you act like you don't like Dom but think I don't know you spent majority of nights there when I was gone." She looked like a deer caught in headlights as I busted her out. I not only had eyes on Tommie while I was gone, but Jasmine as well.

"It's nothing like that. We're just having fun."

"Your fun gon' get that doctor killed."

"What? Why?"

"Because you're playing a dangerous game, and I know Dom not gon' let the shit go on for too long. Shit, honestly, I'm surprised dude's still breathing."

"Dom has no reason to hurt him. We're just friends who are having a good time. He can't get mad at shit I do when he's still fucking different bitches every night."

"Just friends, huh?"

"Yeah, that's it."

"Uh huh. Okay, so tell me, where do 'just friends' chill at? Do y'all be at his apartment he got in the bricks that he takes random hoes to? Or how about his condo that he has for more classier broads? Shit, because that's all 'just friends' would do, don't you agree? He doesn't lay his head at either, so if you made it past both of those, and you lay your head at the same place he lays his head at, then baby sis, you know damn well it's more than just friends. You're wrong as fuck for sleeping with two men anyway. I don't care if he's fucking fifty hoes; you don't try and be like him. Your body is a temple, and you should cherish it and treat it as such."

"Men and these double standards is exactly what Amber Rose be talking about. Shit, shouldn't his dick be sacred and a temple and all that as well?"

"Yeah, but no matter how many hoes we fuck, our dicks will never get run down. They might get burned from fucking with a nasty bitch, but run down? Hell naw. Now you, on the other hand, can ruin ya walls for the next nigga, and for what? All because you wanna be on some 'anything you can do, I can do' type shit? You gon' get pregnant, catch AIDS, and die because somebody else doing it?"

"Whatever, Ghost. Still a double standard, but I see your point. In that case, I'm cutting Dom off."

"Damn, why my nigga had to get the boot?"

"Because unlike Dom, Mark is actually loyal."

"Man, just because he's a blue-collar nigga doesn't mean he's loyal," I said, laughing.

"Actions speak louder than words, and his actions say he's more loyal than Dom."

"Man, get the hell out of here," I said, laughing.

"Anyway, I got a dinner date with my somewhat loyal nigga, so I'ma go freshen up. Love you."

"You need to sit your hot ass down somewhere. Fuck that nigga."

"Hating not a cute look on you, brother," she threw over her shoulder. Laughing, I went into the room to grab some blankets because I planned on catching the couch tonight.

Boom! Boom!

I jumped up with my hand on the trigger of my gun as my eyes tried to focus and adjust to the unfamiliar surroundings. It took me a minute to remember exactly where I was. I was cranky and hung over from downing an entire bottle of alcohol by myself. Combine that with the fact that I was very uncomfortable on this couch made for a very rough night's sleep. Tommie walked into my view and looked a tad bit alarmed to see my gun.

Quickly lowering it, I asked, “What that noise was?”

Rolling her eyes at me, she didn’t answer as she carried a plate of food past me into the room. The shit was smelling good, so I got up and walked inside the kitchen to fix myself a plate only to realize she didn’t cook a nigga shit. Walking out the kitchen into the room, I saw her stuffing her face as she flipped through the channels on TV.

“So you just didn’t fix me any food?”

She continued to eat like I wasn’t talking to her ass at all.

“It’s funny how you the one got the attitude right now like you didn’t disrespect me yesterday by trying to accuse me of doing some foul shit. This role you’re playing has gotten old as hell, and you gon’ find yourself alone in life and very bitter with nine damn cats,” I said as I grabbed clothes and headed into the bathroom.

She must have forgotten who the fuck I was. I had hoes in every area code who would gladly hook a nigga up with a home-cooked meal, but I had no desire to go that route. As I got dressed and handled my hygiene, I just felt drained. I had a lot going on as it was, with my businesses and this whole Henry thing, and now this. This entire ordeal was giving me a fucking headache, and I was more than ready to book a flight back out this bitch. This shit was like a bad ass nightmare I couldn't seem to wake up from.

If I were being honest with myself, I loved the fuck out of Tommie. In the past, I would have never admitted that to myself, but I did. I loved that girl to death. I'd been there when she was at her lowest, doubting herself, and when her self-esteem, self-confidence, and self-worth was all fucked up. I wanted nothing more than to love her, but I wouldn't travel back down that road with her, especially with how she was acting and the slick shit that she was saying lately. I was not feeling it.

I also couldn't wrap my head around the fact if she knew that Rodney and I were cousins or not, but I planned on getting to the bottom of this. I figured that an adult conversation needed to be had, not only man to man but cousin to cousin. I needed that nigga to fully understand this wasn't some bitch I wanted to hit and quit. Regardless if me and Tommie ended up together or not, Royalty was where I drew the line. He couldn't breathe wrong in her direction, or I was killing his ass. I wasn't playing any games when it came to my daughter.

Ever since I saw her on the sonogram screen at Tommie's doctor's appointment and heard her heartbeat, I was sold. Opening the bathroom door, I grabbed my keys and cellphone off the nightstand and headed for the door.

"Where you going?" she asked, but I threw the same silent treatment back at her that she had thrown at me.

"I know you not tryna leave me here, knowing I don't have a car to get around."

"You don't need to go anywhere no way, especially since the doctor said to stay off your feet. Your sister's here too, talk to her."

"Cool, I don't want to talk to your ass no way. I don't need to give you a reason to slap my ass like you did Amber anyway," she said, further trying me. "Cousins of a feather flock together."

"Hell yeah, I knocked her ass the fuck out. The difference between me and the nigga that was beating your ass, I knocked bitches about you; he knocked you out about bitches. It's clear to me you're not ready for a real nigga anyway. What type of man holding his pregnant woman gon' let another chick run up and hit her? So now I'm a woman beater and the bad guy? Fuck you, bruh. You don't wanna deal with a nigga, then say no more," I said as I opened the door to our suite and walked out just as I heard her emotional ass crying, asking me to come back.

Shaking my head at her bipolar ass, I walked down the stairs and out the door. Jogging over to the parking lot, I cursed myself for not valet parking my car. Once I was inside, I pushed the start button, and my car roared to life as I backed out and took off down the street. Hearing my phone ringing, I let my car Bluetooth get it as I pulled off into traffic, headed to my aunt's house.

"Talk to me."

"Who is privy to everything going on in your organization?" Kelina asked.

"Shit, very few people. Why?"

"Because you have a mole. Whoever is feeding information to the Feds is getting it directly from the inside. You might want to link up with those police you have on payroll and get more details, but I hacked into a case file, and they have drop dates, times, amount paid, etcetera. They're not only building a case against you, but Dominic as well. Hell, your entire organization, down to the small-time corner boys. They have it all. This is much bigger than them having someone penetrate your camp. Henry's partner couldn't have gotten all this information.

Nobody even knows where you stay, but it's in here. Somebody in your close inner circle is snitching, and you need to find out who, and fast. This shit is bigger than you think. With so much evidence, I'm clueless as to why you haven't been brought in, and the only thing I can think of is because nothing is really concrete. It doesn't look like you are directly linked to any of the drugs—only a person of high interest. Can you think of anybody who could be feeding them information?" she asked me.

I immediately thought about Tommie and how she randomly popped up, but as soon as that thought came to my mind, it quickly disappeared. She didn't even know what I did, and I left her alone in my house plenty of times, and my safe with books in it that could directly tie me to a lot of shit was always there when I got back. Besides, for nothing else, I knew she was loyal. Hell, she stuck by Rodney's dog ass for years, and with all that he did to her, she never once told me anything about him being a drug dealer. She merely said he beat her ass, and she was the one holding him down all these years. *Who the hell is fucking with me?* I wondered. I was so lost in thought that I had tuned her out until she repeatedly called my name.

"Huh?" I asked, refocusing back on the phone call.

"I said keep your head up and eyes open. I'm here if you need me."

"You don't even know how much I appreciate you right now," I truthfully told her, looking at her in an entirely different light with this newfound information.

"I'ma keep my eyes and ears to the streets and internet world. If I see or hear anything, I'll hit your line up," she said, disconnecting the call.

Kelina was someone that was always looking out for me and was cool as fuck to kick it with; we just never took it further than occasionally fucking. You never know; if she continued to play her cards right, anything could happen.

Appreciative of her looking out for me with that information, I now had even more to add to my plate, but at least I wasn't going into anything blind and had a very even playing field. Knowing what I now knew, I most definitely wasn't staying here a week, and neither was Tommie. I wouldn't leave her here and risk Rodney doing anything to her or my child, or worse, her snake ass friends trying to get revenge. I would dead that hoe, her seed, and her entire fucking family about my child.

That was a side of Ghost these bitches better pray they never saw because I could get all the way retarded when I wanted to. I'd chilled out a lot over the years, mainly because life taught me to think before I reacted and to move smarter and wiser, but they were seriously pushing my fucking buttons and testing me like I wasn't still that nigga.

Pulling into my aunt's driveway, I cut the engine and hopped out of the car. Walking up to the door, I knocked and waited for someone to answer. Being that this was the neighborhood I grew up in, I wasn't worried about anybody trying anything on me as I peeped the corner boys and kids running around.

"My nigga, Ghost," I heard from across the street as my nigga Two Time came jogging over, dapping me up. I had mad love in these streets because I showed love to everybody. I was hard but fair.

"What's up, my nigga? How the kids?"

"They're good. Good looking out last month," he said.

"Shit, it was nothing. Niggas not just gon' try you like that. You're always good in my neck of the woods. I ain't too big that I forgot where I came from or forgot the people who rocked with a nigga tough coming up."

"And that's why I fucks with you. It's good to see you home. Shit, it's been a lil' minute since you touched down in these parts."

"Yeah, you can't stay gone forever."

"Or run from shit forever," he said, and I knew exactly what he was talking about, but I wasn't getting into that right now.

"Man, gone 'head with that," I said.

"Well, get up with me before your leave," he said, dapping me off one last time before walking off, back across the street. Turning back around to the house, I rang the doorbell. I noticed a car in the yard, so I knew my aunt had to be here. Figuring the doorbell might be broken, I knocked a few more times but harder than the first and, again, waited to see if someone came to the door.

"Got damn it, hold on! I'm coming!" a voice yelled, followed by locks being turned. "Who the hell beating on my door like the police?" my aunt asked as she swung the door open. Once her eyes landed on me, she immediately jumped with joy and practically knocked me down trying to get to me. "My baby is home!" she squealed, kissing me all over my face.

My aunt was more like my mother than anything. Being the older of her and my birth mother, when her baby sister turned to drugs, she took it upon herself to take me in and raise me as her own, and she never loved me any less. She raised Rodney and I as if we were brothers; that was why that fight really cut me deep.

Walking inside her home, everything looked the same as I remembered it down to the TVs and furniture. As Rodney's plug, I knew he was seeing big faces, so the fact that nothing changed about the home, not even the location, didn't sit too well with me. I almost thought for a split second that when the door opened, I would be told I had the wrong address. Closing the door behind her, I walked into the kitchen and took a seat at the table. She had it smelling really good in here, and I couldn't wait to get a plate.

"Why didn't you tell me you was coming into town? I would have fixed my baby his favorite food."

"To be honest, it was a spur of the moment thing. I didn't know I was coming into town until early yesterday morning."

"What's going on? You in trouble or something?"

"My lady was in the hospital, and I took the first plane I could."

"Is she okay?" she asked with a concerned expression of her wrinkle-free face.

"Yeah, Aunt Louise, her and the baby are fine."

"Baby? See, you and your damn brother gon' give me a heartache. First, he's running around here acting like he wasn't raised right, doing that poor girl like that. You know he brought some hussy around here the other day, talking about he wants to marry her? He acts like I don't know what he was doing to Tommie. That's why he never wanted to bring her to the house anymore, but a mother always knows. Every time I saw that sweet girl, I knew," she said, shaking her head as if she had failed at life. She had this faraway look in her eyes as if she were reminiscing about something. "I think I was too lenient with you boys. I gave y'all a good ass whooping, but hell, I don't know. Now, you got a baby on the way, and you never even told me you had a girlfriend. I'm excited about being a grandmother, though, and I hope you plan on doing right by this girl because a baby is such a beautiful thing. When do I get to meet this mystery lady who's made me a grandmother at such an early age anyway?" she asked, tucking her hair behind her ear.

Looking at her, I knew I had to gon' and tell her everything that was going on. I would hate for her to get caught up in this mess, but I knew it had to be done. I opened my mouth to speak just as the door opened, and I heard, “Ma where you at?” as Rodney came walking in with Karter.

CHAPTER 4

RODNEY

"So the nigga snuck you?" Mike asked as he sat across from me inside of Burger King.

"Hell yeah, his punk ass did that sucker ass shit," I said as I watched Karter playing inside the kiddie play area. I didn't know how much longer I was going to lie to myself about that being my seed. The lil' nigga looked just like me.

"Daddy, look at me," he said, running to the slide and going down. A huge smile formed on my face just watching him. I somewhat now regretted all the time I'd missed with him, chasing hoes and choosing Tommie's fat, disloyal ass over him.

"Man, shit's not adding the fuck up. Why would he just hit you out the blue like that?" Mike asked, rubbing his chin. "You said something crazy to him or somethin'? You know how your slick ass mouth can be. Ghost is usually more level headed than that unless a nigga tries him.

"Ghost's usually more level headed than that," I said, mimicking him. "Nigga, get the fuck out of here." In the past, when he used to dick ride Ghost, I would just let the shit ride, but today, I was very annoyed by the shit, like hop off this nigga's dick. "Nigga, you sound like you siding with him or some shit, talking about *what you say to him*."

"Man, get that bass out yo' voice and calm yo' ass the fuck down. I'm just trying to figure how the nigga came to sneak yo' ass out the blue if a conversation wasn't even had. Shit, you getting defensive and doing that extra shit not even called for."

"Nigga, you think if I knew the answer to that shit, I would be sitting here, looking confused as fuck?" I yelled, clearly downplaying the situation. I told Mike after he came and scooped me up that Ghost's ass had snuck me and put me out the car.

Shit, I was still trying to wrap my head around the events that had transpired. Never in a million years did I see this shit coming. My brother and my ex-bitch were fucking. I didn't care about her fat ass at first, but seeing her pregnant and glowing, I felt some type of way that my brother could possibly be fucking her and the reason for that glow. Her actually being pregnant still had me feeling some type of way, and combining that to the fact that this nigga really thought he was gon' raise my damn child, like he had me all kinds of fucked up. I knew I didn't want the kid at first, but his ass didn't need to know that.

"Well, how the hell you ended up with Karter? Y'all was at Amber's house when he put you out? I thought you didn't even go over there in the daytime like that?"

"Nigga, the fuck is this? An interrogation? You Sherlock Holmes or some shit? Damn! I got Karter because some nigga Amber's dirty hoe ass was fucking with knocked her ass the fuck out, so I was headed to get my seed," I said, lying through my teeth. I was gon' play this kid out for as long as I could.

"Shit, I can't even feel bad, because that hoe been bogus, so it's about time somebody put her on her ass. Shit, I hope you ain't beat dude's ass either; you need to find that nigga and match a blunt with him," he said, picking up his whopper and taking a bite. Did I feel bad that Ghost knocked my baby momma the fuck out? Shit, hell naw, because nobody told her goofy ass to run up and try and hit Tommie.

I was glad Ghost knocked her out before I could because I saw her getting up to hit Tommie; that was why I was walking over there. I couldn't even explain the shit. It was like I could beat her ass and talk shit to her, but another person couldn't try that shit. It had nothing to do with me seeing her and wanting her back—well, at least that was what I was going to tell myself. I guess the saying was true: you don't want somebody until somebody else has them. Hearing my phone ringing, I looked down, noticing Amber calling me.

"What you want?"

"Where the fuck is my son at? And tell your cousin this shit ain't over. I got some niggas that's gon' fuck him up, so his best bet is to hop a plane back home."

"Bitch, you got some niggas that will die right along with your simple ass, so shit, do what you feel, but my son not gon' be around when you do it."

"You sound like a straight bitch. First, you let the nigga beat your ass, take your bitch, and then knock your baby momma out in front of your child. You ain't shit and still taking up for him. You should have your men run down on his ass, but instead, you over there telling me to watch my back like this nigga the boogie man or some shit. Fuck you, Rodney, and bring me my damn son before I blow your spot the fuck up. Try me if you want to, like I don't know you got Kelly living in the same house Tommie was living in."

That's where the silly bitch always went wrong—thinking she knew every damn thing. Kelly hadn't even moved inside the house yet and was currently still at the condo, but I wasn't about to tell her ass any different. I was gon' let her go to my crib and clown so the neighbors could call the laws. They didn't play that shit in that neighborhood.

"Listen here, you ran through bitch. I done let you get away with damn near murder over the years because I felt partially responsible for taking your virginity and fucking with you for a few months then wifing your best friend instead. I let you say and do anything as long as you didn't get out of line and knew your place. Shit, I didn't trip on what you did or who you did it with. Let's not act like you wasn't out here running through niggas like they were going out of style. Still, I let that shit slide. I never beat your ass, never even pushed you, and that's where I fucked up at. Had I been going upside your head like Tommie's, yo' ass would know who the fuck not to play with. You a bad bitch, so go ahead and try your luck, bitch, and on my momma, they'll never find your fucking body. You think I give a fuck about you when I damn near beat Tommie to death, and she been rocking with a nigga for years? Fuck with it if you want to, Amber. You'll get my son back when I feel like giving him the fuck back," I said before I hung up on her ass.

"You seem to have your hands full. So if you not giving him back, what you gon' do? Take him home with you?" he asked. Thinking it over, I realized he was right. I couldn't spring him on Kelly like that. I mean, I could, but I wanted to ease the topic in first. Until then, it was really only one place I could take him, so I had to prepare myself for the ass whooping moms was gon' give me for bringing her grandson around four years later.

"Take me to get my car. I'ma just go to my house tonight since Kelly's at the condo, and tomorrow, I'll go to Mom's house. I got a long day ahead of me tomorrow. Hell, I need to check on this deal in Jersey and try and find a new connect."

"Now, hold up. It's one thing for you and Ghost to fight, but now, you're tryna leave and find a new connect? Shit's going too far when you know he got the best prices and purest shit. Who else gon' give us shit like that?"

"Hell, I don't know. It's other plugs around. I heard of this cat out of Houston—Midos—and word is he got some good ass product."

"Shit, is his shit pure like Ghost's, and is he gon' let them bricks go for as cheap as Ghost does? Because the team can't afford to receive less money all because you putting personal shit before business."

"Nigga, just drive me to my shit. You forgot this is my empire; I make sure everybody's eating, so as long as they still eating, shouldn't nobody say shit," I said, walking off to go get Karter. I hated to admit that he was right, because nobody could touch Ghost's ass with what he supplied us with, and he had doubled our supply intake for little to nothing. Shit, he was practically giving me the shit really, but I was on some 'fuck Ghost' type shit right now and in my feelings, so I was gon' still try and set a meeting up with Midos anyways. You never knew until you tried. I didn't think there was any coming back from today.

"Daddy, whose house is this?" Karter asked as we pulled up to my mom's house the next day. Last night was my first night keeping him not only overnight but alone overnight, and that shit was no joke. I needed one of those damn *Raising Kids for Dummies* books or something if I planned to make this a normal thing. I thought the shit was easy since mothers made it look easy, but I got a rude awakening last night.

"This is your grandma's house."

"Nu uh, 'cause my glamma Jenny lives that a way," he said, pointing in the opposite direction. "And ha house not look like this."

"What the hell is a glamma?" I asked him as he stared blankly at me. "Never mind, I don't even know why I asked you," I mumbled as I put the car in park and got out. I had started walking to the door before I realized he hadn't gotten out. *Shit, this parenting thing gon' take some getting used to*, I thought as I quickly went to open his door. I had to put the child lock on after his bad ass kept opening it, trying to look down at the road as I drove. Walking inside the house, I called out to my mother, "Ma, where you at?" as I headed toward the kitchen because something smelled good as hell. When my eyes landed on Ghost, my jaw immediately tensed up, and I had the urge to rush this nigga.

"That's the man who you was fighting, Daddy," Karter said, pointing at Ghost.

Looking from Karter, to me, and to Ghost, my mother didn't know what to say. I knew with one look at Karter, she knew he was mine, so I knew she was feeling some type of way about that. Then, the little shit just had to snitch about the fight.

"What the fuck is going on? Rodney Jeremiah Daniels, I know like hell this isn't your child I'm looking at. I know it. I know my eyes are playing tricks on me because if not, I'm about two seconds from hopping across this table onto your yellow ass," she said, mad as hell. I knew she would feel some type of way, but damn, she was looking like she wanted to catch a fade with a nigga or some shit.

"Listen, Ma, I can explain everything."

Turning the knob off on the stove, she turned back around with her arms folded and said, "Get to explaining then."

"I didn't know for a fact that he was mine; that's why I didn't bring him around until I was certain," I said, which was partially true. The other reason was her ass was team Tommie and would have, for sure, snitched on my ass.

I looked at Karter, and he was having this intense stare down with Ghost with his little fists balled up. This little nigga was something serious. You would've thought he had forgotten what happened yesterday, or was at least scared, but he had a look on his face that said if he was a little bigger, he would have caught a fade by now. I didn't know if I wanted to be mad at Amber's ghetto ass for his behavior or a proud parent because my little homie didn't take any shit off anybody and was with all of that dumb shit. I knew I would never receive any phone calls about him being bullied on the playground.

"Why's he staring at your cousin like that?" my momma asked because even she had noticed it. Walking over to Karter, she kneeled down and said, "Hey, handsome. What is your name?"

"I no like him," my son said, pointing to Ghost, who just smirked. I swear, if this nigga said some out the way shit to my seed, we were turning this kitchen upside down.

"Why not, baby?"

"'Cause him not nice," my baby said, playing with his shirt now that the spotlight was solely on him. Looking around, he locked eyes with me and walked back over to where I was, grabbing my leg and holding onto it.

"Of all the things you've ever done, Rodney, this shit takes the cake. Talking about you wasn't sure if that was your baby. I have an entire photo album that would beg to differ. That little boy is the spitting image of you," she said, glaring at me. When her eyes landed on Karter, her facial expressions softened up as she said, "Rodney was is this child's name?" She asked me with an attitude.

"Karter," I said to her. Giving me an evil look, her eyes landed back on Karter as her face softened and Karter, are you hungry?" She asked him in the sweetest voice.

He looked up at me as if to ask for confirmation, and when I nodded, he said, "Yes."

"Granny's going to fix you something to eat. Come on, baby. Let's get you washed up," she said, walking over and grabbing his hand.

"If you my grandma, then who is my glamma Jenny?" Karter asked as they walked off. My mother turned to look at me when he mentioned glamma, and I just shrugged because, shit, I didn't know either. Once they left, I just stared at Ghost's ass, not bothering to take a seat or even look away. I had to let this nigga know what it was and that I wasn't scared of him. The nigga pumped fear in everybody else's heart, but I wasn't going for the shit. He put on his pants one pants leg at a time just like me. Just then, Momma and Karter came walking back into the kitchen, smiling and laughing. It warmed my heart that my mom took to him that quickly. I knew she would love him unconditionally. Judging by the way he was smiling, he liked her as well.

"And the space alien had come to my room, but I beat him up," Karter was saying as he bounced around while she made him cereal.

"He did?" my mom asked, faking like she was surprised.

"Uh huh, and it was a big monster, but I told my mommy *I'll protect you*, so I started beating him up like this," he said, punching the air with his little fists. I just laughed at his ass because he was truly a character.

"Aye, once you start him to talking, he'll go all day," I said, laughing.

"Speaking of Mommy, who is his? Because I know it's not Tommie?" she asked the million-dollar question.

"Tommie? Her my god mommy, and they got into a fight," Karter said. "And him, him hit my mommy," he said, pointing at Ghost.

At that exact moment, Ghost stood up as if he were about to walk out, and her head quickly snapped in his direction. "Landon Isaiah Carter, don't you even fucking try it. You better sit your ass down before I knock you down. I know like hell you didn't hit no female."

"Damn, auntie, a nigga was just going to the bathroom. I ain't leaving, because this conversation needs to be had because what I won't do is fucking repeat myself," he said, looking dead at me when he said that. I was tired of this nigga thinking he was scaring me or some shit. Yeah, he'd gotten the best of me yesterday because he caught me off guard, but let's be clear, the nigga didn't just beat my ass. He just got the most licks.

There wasn't any bitch in my blood, so when he said that shit, I said, "Nigga, don't throw fucking slurs and shit like a bitch! Get the shit off your chest then," I yelled, moving Karter to the side just in case he wanted to do something.

He pulled his pants up and lunged at me, catching me on the side of my jaw. I countered with a powerful punch of my own, and we took off, going lick for lick.

Karter picked up his bowl and threw it at Ghost and then grabbed the dust pan and started hitting him with it. If the situation hadn't been as serious as it was, I would have started laughing at his little ass trying to help me jump this nigga.

"Get off my daddy, bitch!" Karter yelled.

"Don't you dare be cursing in my house. I'll tear your little ass up," Ma Dukes said, popping him on his hands. "Rodney, cut that shit out in front of your child!" she yelled at me like I was the only one fighting. She always did that, like her precious Landon could do no wrong. However, hearing her voice, I stopped fighting until this nigga threw a mean ass combo at me. Our entire life, that nigga had always been a good fighter and should have went out for boxing or some shit because his hands were past decent, and that right hook would've put anyone on their ass, but still, I wasn't that same nine-year-old kid needing my big cousin to fight for me. I wasn't taking any shit, so I shook back from those hits and started back throwing punches of my own.

I wasn't one to fight, but I was a beast with a gun and never missed, but shit, that didn't mean I couldn't fight; I just preferred to fight with a bullet. I was too pretty for the extra bullshit. Stepping back, I swung, and he ducked and came back with a lick that put me on my ass as I fell over the chair and broke it into pieces.

"Stop it! Stop it! Landon, Rodney, y'all stop this shit right fucking now! Y'all tearing my damn house up!" my momma yelled, hitting us both on the top of our heads with brooms at the same time as Karter kicked Ghost in his lower legs since that was all he could reach. My mom saw this and started popping my ass harder with the broom then switched and started hitting Ghost's ass. She was literally going to town on our asses, but I felt like she was mainly popping my ass instead of this big ass nigga.

"Alright, Mama damn," I said, and she popped my ass again as Ghost started laughing, so she turned and smacked his ass as well.

"Next one of y'all who makes a fucking move will be visiting Heaven earlier than expected. Y'all better calm the fuck down. Got my blood pressure all up dealing with this shit. Y'all carrying on like this in my house that I pay bills and acting crazy in front of a child like you wasn't raised right. I'm disappointed in both of y'all, but especially you, Rodney. You need to be more focused on being a parent for this damn child cursing in my house like he's grown and jumping in grown folk's shit. Back in my day, a child knew their place and how to behave. You need to focus on raising him right instead of running around sticking your little thing in anything that fucking moves. Now, I'm about to get this child situated upstairs, and when I come back down, somebody better get to fucking talking, or I'm going upside both y'all heads again," she said, breathing heavily up and down. I got up and went to the bathroom, which was to the right of the kitchen, and slammed the door.

"And you better stop fucking slamming my damn door like you paying bills around this bitch!" she yelled. I paid her no mind because she quickly forgot that I did pay bills around this bitch. I was always stopping by to lace her with some bread. Examining my eye, I noticed it was starting to swell. If that nigga and I locked up again, I was shooting his ass.

"So which one of y'all wanna go first?" my momma asked. We were sitting around her table, and she was looking from me to Ghost.

"I met a girl a few months ago, and she looked like somebody had been using her as a punching bag. She said she had to flee the state because her boyfriend had tried to beat her baby out of her. She never said a name or where she was from. I fell in love with her and found out a few days ago that she came home to see about her moms and collapsed. That girl is Tommie, and she's carrying my little girl. Biologically, she's his, but that's all the claim he has on her. That's my baby, and I won't hesitate to protect her with my life, regardless if me and Tommie be together or not," he said looking at me.

Turning to me, my mom reached back and slapped the shit out of me.

"What the fuck, Ma?" I yelled, grabbing my face as she slapped me again.

"Watch your mouth in my house, and how dare you beat that girl half to death? I didn't raise you to put your hands on women, yet you stayed putting your hands on that girl. Yeah, don't look surprised; I saw all the signs. My only regret is not stepping in. You are just like your father. He used to beat the hell out of me just for fun and stayed putting me down. He broke me so far down that, shit, I didn't even know what it felt like to stand up. First, it was the mental abuse. *You're getting fat, you need to put that burger down, you're ugly, no man will ever want you, I'm the only one that wants your ass,* and so on. Then came the psychical abuse. I saw all the signs in that poor girl, yet I'd turned a blind eye. I feel just as responsible," she said with her head down. We all sat there for a moment in silence as I absorbed what she'd revealed about my father. *Was I my father's child?*

"Landon, I'm upset that you and your cousin were fighting, but baby, I don't blame you."

"What!" I yelled.

"You heard me. You have no right putting your hands on that girl, and he didn't know that was your ex, but it doesn't matter even if he did. One man's trash can easily become another man's treasure. You see her doing good; now you wanna try and miss her. I don't know where I went wrong with you, boy, but you better get right, and fast. A blind man can see your cousin loves that girl and that baby she's carrying, and I won't stand in his way while he tries to do right by that baby who didn't ask to be here. You were man enough to make it, you should be man enough to raise it."

"You're my momma, and you gon' side with him? Oh, but why am I not surprised? Your precious Ghost can do no wrong," I said, throwing my hands up.

"You are child, my only son, and I love you more than life itself, but I won't uplift you when you are wrong."

"This not a damn competition. This is someone's life and the life of a child. The extra shit? I don't give a fuck about that extra shit. Me and Tommie not even rocking like that right now since she found out we're related, but that won't stop me from loving *my* daughter. You lost your rights the minute you tried to beat the baby out of her. Shit, you wanna beef? Cool. As long as you don't play with the business aspect, then I'm fine with that because I wouldn't dare do some fuck shit like pull your product, but don't fucking try me about my money, because shit gon' get real. You got five hundred thou in product of mine, and I expect it returned or my half of the money from sales. Try me if you want to," he said calmly, getting up, kissing my mom on her forehead and leaving out.

"You fix this, Rodney, and you fix it now. Stop whatever you have planned and are doing because you know how passionate he gets when he feels strongly about something. You gave that girl up; take your loss and move on."

"You're saying that like I'm supposed to be scared of that nigga. He's bleeding like I'm bleeding!" I yelled, getting up. I headed upstairs and grabbed Karter up. The reason I brought him was for my mom to keep him, but now, that shit was out the question. With how I was feeling right now, Kelly's ass could get with the program, or I'd move another bitch in who would jump at the chance to watch the lil' nigga. Walking back downstairs, my mom sat rocking back and forth. "I don't want to bury my son."

"Bye, Granny," Karter said, giving her a hug.

"Bye, Granny's baby. You gon' cut that cursing out?"

He nodded his head.

"You better, or Granny gon' tear them legs up."

"How you figure you'll be burying me and not Ghost?" I asked her. She stared at me blankly, giving me all the confirmation that I needed. She had more faith in Ghost than me. Well, I was gon' show her. I was gon' show everybody who doubted a nigga, including Ghost. They were gon' regret ever sleeping on me.

"Because I buried your father," she said to my back as I walked out of the house.

CHAPTER 5

TOMMIE

"Ten, nine, eight, seven, six, five, four, three, two, one! Happy New Year!" the crowd cheered as everyone went wild. Jasmine had brought me to Times Square to watch the ball drop, and I must say I'd never experienced anything like that in my entire life.

"Happy New Year, baby sis. My New Year's resolution is to do better as a person and get a better grip on my situationships."

"Situationships with an s? Damn, bitch, I'm out here struggling to get one man, and you got many," I told her, and this idiot popped an imaginary collar.

"Naw, I'm kidding, but I do want to just enjoy life and live it like it's my last. I also want us to form a closer bond and for my niece to come out cute as a button because, I'm telling you now, I can't claim no ugly baby," she said with her hands on her hips. Speaking of New Year's wishes and resolutions, I decided to give mine. Closing my eyes, I said a quick prayer.

Dear God, it's me, Tommie. Well, I didn't have to say my name, because I'm sure you automatically knew it was me. I've been praying to you so much every night, you probably have my repetitive words memorized. I've just had a bad year is all, like 2016 just wasn't for me, but I have faith 2017 will be better. I just have a few wishes and requests. I know you have other people to tend to, so I won't be selfish and take up all your time. I'll keep this brief. First, I'm so very thankful to be allowed to see 2017 because lying in that hospital bed, I almost didn't make it. This year, I just want to regain my happiness and find peace and love because I've lost all three. I also want this anger removed from my heart because, God, I'm still very much angry and, sometimes, unintentionally lash out at the wrong people. I feel so worthless, betrayed, and just not good enough. I pray you allow me to find my way back, and I hope I'm not too far gone. I pray you show me if Landon is for me. Just in case you get confused, he also goes by Ghost. Send me a sign, showing me which direction I should take, and could you make sure it's an easy to read sign? Because you know I can sometimes have my slow moments. Well, you know this because you see and hear everything from up high. Also, can you let me have a painless delivery of Royalty because I was watching the pregnancy channel, and I just cannot do that. I'd be very appreciative if you just allowed her to slide on out. Thank you, God, for taking the time out to listen to me. Oh, P.S., may my snapback be the truth? Amen

Opening my eyes, I glanced around at all the smiling couples and happy people and craved to feel that same joyful feeling soon.

"Bitch, it's cold as hell. Let's go get some food," Jas said, taking ahold of my hand and walking with me through the crowd, back toward the opposite direction.

"You know me oh so well," I said at the thought of food that made my mouth water. My ass stayed hungry all day, every day.

Back in the car, I grabbed my purse, which I left inside, and picked my phone up out of it to check my messages. Of all the happy New Year's texts, one stood out—a message from Ghost.

Damn, God, that was fast, I thought to myself.

Tell my daughter I said I love her and Happy New Years was what the text read. Immediately replying, I said. *I'll tell her, but that's all who you wanted to wish Happy New Years and an I love you to?* Pressing send, I eagerly waited for a response as we drove in search of food. Two hours later, as I lie in my bed holding my phone, realizing that I still had not received one, I came to the conclusion that one wasn't coming. I guess this was my sign, loud and clearly. I guess the saying was true: be careful what you wish for because you just might get it. Putting my phone down, I closed my eyes and drifted off to sleep, feeling more alone than ever.

Take me to the king
I don't have much to bring
My heart is torn in pieces
It's my offering
Take me to the king
Truth is I'm tired
Options are few
I'm trying to pray
But where are you?
I'm all churched out
Hurt and abused
I can't fake

What's left to do?

Truth is I'm weak

No strength to fight

No tears to cry

Even if I tried

But still my soul

Refuses to die

One touch-will change-my life

Take me to the king

I don't have much to bring

My heart's torn into pieces

It's my offering

Singing along with Tamela Mann, I busied myself around the house, cleaning up as best as I could. It had been two months since everything went down in Atlanta. Since then, I had decided to come back to New York because Atlanta just held too many bad memories for me, and I would rather be with Jasmine and Ghost than in Atlanta. They'd moved my mother to a cancer treatment facility, and it happened to only be two hours from me—an hour and a half really with how my driver drove. I had a personal driver since Ghost insisted I didn't need to revert to taking Ubers, especially since the weather was so bad lately.

Speaking of him, I missed him so much, especially at night time when I craved his touch, rubbing my belly until I would fall asleep. My own stubbornness was what pushed him away. I tried to address the New Year's incident, but he barely said two words to me aside from checking on the baby, so I guess it really was over.

My therapist thought I needed to focus on getting myself together and dealing with my insecurities first before I could be the woman Ghost needed. It pissed me off because I'd done this song and dance before. I did let go. I was the woman he needed. I'd just had a relapse. Apparently, you weren't allowed to have one of those, because suddenly, everyone thought I was crazy. Maybe being alone would be good for me. Maybe Ghost and I weren't meant to be.

Each day was a struggle, trying to make my heart not want something it had been yearning for, but I made my own bed, and I would just have to lie in it. Like the saying said: if you love someone, let them go, and if they come back, then it was meant to be.

Satisfied with how tidy everything was, I went to the back to get dressed and start my day. I was in a cheerful mood, so I decided to go and do some shopping for Royalty even though her little ass had everything the mall, Target, and online stores had to offer, but hey, maybe there would be a new selection today. She would be making her debut soon, and I was more than excited to meet my baby and ready for her to vacate my stomach. I loved her very much, but it was eviction time, and her ass was always on my bladder and wouldn't let me sleep. She had to go.

Texting my driver to let him know my plans, I was in the process of putting my phone down when I noticed I had a few notifications on Facebook. Clicking on the app, I saw Rodney had tagged me in this long apology post that had gotten three thousand likes, over four thousand shares, and had basically gone viral. Not bothering to read the post, I clicked on my messages and noticed he had also slid in my inbox, asking for my number, and called himself checking on his daughter. He even left his contact information as if I would use the shit! Not even bothering to reply, I deleted and blocked him.

I was proud of myself because had this been last month or any time before, I possibly would have replied back and also accepted his apology because, ultimately, that was all I ever wanted. I did forgive him, though, only because Dr. Phil suggested I forgave him—not for him but for Royalty and myself so that I could let that negative energy go. I realized how much negativity I projected onto Ghost way before that blow up in Atlanta. Making a post of my own, I kept it simple and said,

Now you thinking about the fuck shit that you shouldn't have did, but I won't ever take you back, so no need to play and pretend. You was sleep, thinking real niggas wasn't choosing. You played ya hand, but I'm sorry, fuck nigga, you are losing.

As soon as I posted it, I received twenty likes in literally one minute. I didn't do Facebook, so I clicked off the app and put my phone down. I was sure somebody would screenshot my status and send it to him.

"Tommie!" I heard my name being called.

"I'm in my room," I said to my sister. I was still staying with Jas mainly because I didn't want to stay alone, and I loved her house. I did have plans on moving out, though.

"Hey, big momma," she said, walking in and rubbing my belly.

"Hey, boo."

"What you 'bout to get into?"

"Headed to the mall to do a little shopping for Royalty."

"Good, thank God you're going. Now I don't have to beg and plead my case to get you to go with me," she said, smiling.

"But why would you have had to do all of that?"

"Shit, your big ass never wants to do anything but sulk around the house and eat ever since New Year's and that whole 'Ghost not texting back' dilemma. By the way, you have nobody to blame for losing Ghost but yourself. I've been meaning to have a talk with you. That man loves you."

I rolled my eyes as she said that.

"He does, regardless of what he's been running around doing or who he's doing it with. He loves you, and instead of letting that man love you, you pushed him away and made him feel not only like you rejected his love but also blamed him for another man's actions. If he up and marries somebody else, you have no one to blame but yourself. You lost a good ass man, who was not only willing to love you past the hurt and pain but also accepted your child and loves that baby as if she came from him. You know how many women in your position would kill for a man like that? Yeah, you suffered a traumatic experience, but you survived. You fell down, but you got back up again. You can't let your circumstances define who you are as a person. Now you're alone and miserable. It wasn't worth it, sis, and you was wrong," she scolded.

I knew she was right, but damn, she didn't have to be so harsh and hurt my damn feelings.

"Damn, you could have said it in a nicer way," I said, tearing up.

"Don't you dare cry. This is some tough love for your ass. I'm not your friend; I'm your big sister, so I gotta tell you what's right and give you the raw truth. You fucked up—not that man. You, Tommie. Shit, he fought his family because of you, and you gon' accuse him of being foul and say 'oh you gon' beat me too.' You're mad wrong." Putting my head down in shame, I had no words for my actions. I knew I had messed up, and that realization was gon' fuck with me for the rest of my life if I lost him for good.

"I know, sis. My pride just won't allow me to apologize."

"That's fine, but your pride will allow you to be alone in life, baby girl. But enough of that. Come on so we can go."

"I have a car picking me up."

"Ghost got you spoiled as hell," she said, laughing. "But that's even better because I hate driving in this weather with these no driving ass folks. Looks like I'm getting chauffeured around today."

Walking around the mall, going from store to store, I said, "What are we even looking for if we found your outfit a while ago?"

"We're looking for you something to wear."

"I'm big as hell. Where the hell could I possibly go?"

"Ghost and Dom are opening up another clothing store, and it's their grand opening Friday night."

"Definitely not going," I said, turning around to head toward the food court.

"Yes, you are. Dad is going to be there as well. It's a family affair. Family supports family, no matter what."

"Don't feed me that family bullshit. You just want to go because Dom is going to be there. Let's not act like he didn't cut you off, because he texted me a while ago, saying he was done playing games with you," I said, busting her out.

Folding her arms and pouting, she said, "It's not fair he gets to do his own thing, but I'm supposed to just not have a life and wait around until he decides to give me some time and dick?"

"You can live your life; you just can't have any outside dick."

"That's not fucking fair."

"That's life, big sis."

"Well, it's not my life. If he can't give me a full commitment—mind, body, and soul—then he don't get no faithful pussy. Besides, it's not that I'm fucking random guys, and Mark doesn't even live here, so technically, I am faithful," she said, shrugging. "Well, when I'm not in Atlanta."

"Shit, you're a mess. How you gon' give me advice just now? You need to take your own advice," I said, laughing.

"No, my situation is different. Dominic's mad because I don't chase him and act crazy on his ass like all them other hoes. He wants a bitch who's gon' run up behind him, jump out of bushes, slash his tires, and blow his phone up. Shit, I be getting dicked down. I don't have time to stalk him. I catch flights, not feelings," she said. I looked at her like *girl, bye*.

"Bitch, you may have not caught feelings in the past, but your ass is most definitely in your feelings behind this nigga."

"Shit, I think I'm dickmatized," she said as I started laughing at her. "Oh no, don't do me, baby, because let's not act like you stayed with Rodney for his cooking," she said.

"That was low, bitch," I said as I quickly stopped laughing because it was true. The way he worked his hips when he was deep inside of me should have been illegal—had me taking ass whippings and cursing my damn self out like *bitch, you done got us in trouble, and we might not get no dick tonight.*

"Let's get off sex because my hormones are at an all-time high right now. I could literally rape a nigga," I said miserably as I had a flashback of the bomb ass head Ghost threw on me a few months ago. Just thinking about it and that monster I saw that he was working with made me want to beat whoever's ass he was fucking with now—not because I had beef but because I was mad she was getting something I craved but had yet to have. I could only imagine what the sex was like.

"Damn, bitch, you're drooling and shit. What the hell was you just thinking about?" she asked, laughing.

Embarrassed, I wiped my mouth. "Umm, nothing. Some food," I quickly said.

"Uh huh. Anyway, back to what I was saying. Are you going Friday night?"

"What if Ghost has a date?" I whined because I didn't think my heart could take it.

"He will. He and Kelina have gotten a lot closer. And before you ask, no, I haven't beat the bitch up, but I did let Ghost know I wouldn't play about you if she got out of pocket, but I couldn't blame him for choosing her."

I whipped my head around so fast to look at her like she had sprouted two heads. "Really, Jas?"

"Yes, really. While you were busy being selfish, you never stopped to ask if he had stuff going on as well, which he does. It's so much shit that's jumped off. I'm surprised he's still functioning. A lesser man would have folded, but Ghost is built Ford tough."

"What's going on?" I asked because he didn't talk to me anymore if it wasn't about Royalty.

"Too much for lil' ole me to explain, but the Feds is watching."

"He's going to jail!" I yelled so loudly that people paused to observe me.

My heart felt like it was breaking into a million pieces. My chest tightened up, and I felt as if I would pass out any minute now.

"Look, I'm telling you about his situation and Kelina so you can already be prepared and not act like you're acting right now. Get it all out because you'll never again let a soul see you sweat—not even that nigga. You dealt with Rodney, so you know what comes with the game," she said. Now, I was confused because Ghost was a business man, and Rodney was a drug dealer. Those were two different situations. *Maybe he's been embezzling money or something?*

She continued talking, interrupting my thoughts. "He's my brother, and you are my sister. I love you both dearly, and I'm caught in the middle, so I'm staying out of it. This is for you guys to work out. However, I will say give it some time and learn to do your own thing. Well, after you drop this load," she said, laughing and rubbing my stomach. I did a fake laugh too as I became consumed with my own thoughts again.

Had my own insecurities really pushed the man I love into the arms of another woman, and could I handle seeing that? Those were the real questions. Was I really that selfish that I ignored his own battles?

CHAPTER 6

JASMINE

"Shit," I said as I felt my tire blow on the highway as I swerved to avoid hitting a car then veered off to the shoulder and put the car in park. Glancing up, I saw that I was maybe a quarter of a mile from the exit, which had a gas station on the corner. May

be I could get some Fix-A-Flat that would allow me to make it home. Getting out the car, wearing nothing but some jeggings and long-sleeve turtle-neck shirt with a peacoat and light brown Uggs, I walked around to the blown tire on the passenger side of my car.

Examining it closer, I saw that I couldn't go anywhere on it without risking damaging my axel. My tire was completely blown open in several different places. I couldn't even slow creep up the street. "Fuck!" I yelled in frustration as I quickly got back inside my car. "I do not need this bullshit right now!" I screamed. It was midnight, and I was headed back from Walmart, getting Tommie's fat ass some snacks.

I sure had a mouthful for Ghost when I spoke to his ass again because he wanted to play daddy and shit, so he needed to keep up with these cravings, had me running around in the middle of the night for cookie-dough ice cream, a jar of dill pickles, already made up Kool-Aid to dip them in, hot Cheetos, and baby powder. The doctor said her iron may have been low, thus the strange craving for baby powder. Not only was she addicted to the stuff like crack, she was only addicted to a certain kind and would throw a fit if it weren't the right one.

Pulling my insurance card out of my glove compartment, I called Triple A and gave them all my information only to find out that they were backed up tonight, and it would be nearly two hours before they could reach me. Quickly calling Ghost back to back until he answered, I said, "Ghost, I need you right now," as soon as the phone connected.

"Hello?" a female voice answered, catching me off guard. I had to pull the phone away from my ear to make sure I had even dialed the right number.

"Hello?" she repeated, this time with an attitude. I knew this hoe didn't.

"Put Ghost on the phone," I said, getting straight to the point. I wasn't sure whether this was Kelina or not and didn't really care at the moment.

"Excuse you?"

"Bitch, you're excused! Now quit fucking talking to me and put my brother on the phone now!" I yelled.

"Who the fuck told you to answer my shit?" I heard Ghost ask.

"Well, it kept ringing."

"I don't give a fuck if it rung a hundred times, back to back, that doesn't give you the right to answer my shit. Go in the living room and sit the fuck down."

"Ghost!" I yelled into the phone to get his attention. I appreciated that he was checking this bitch, but he needed to do it on his own time because I was stuck. It was dark, late, and getting colder by the second. I needed to get off this highway and to my house.

"Jasmine?"

"Yeah, I need your fucking help and this is all your fault," I said, going in on him.

"Slow down. What's all my fault, and what you need help with?"

"I'm stuck because your fat ass baby momma wanted a list of snacks, and I went to go get them in the cold, and now, I've had a blowout. Triple A said it will take nearly two hours to reach me, and you know Momma and Daddy went to Milwaukee and won't be back until sometime tomorrow before the grand opening. This is your fault. That's your baby momma, and you should be catering to cravings. You're slacking," I said.

"No, I'm not slacking. Her ass knows who to ask because she knows I wouldn't get the shit. She is not even supposed to be eating none of that, especially that damn powder. I know that's mainly what she asked you to get. She gon' make me beat her ass," he said, pausing. "How is she?"

"You would know if you came by to check on her instead of just texting here and there."

"Man, I know. A nigga gotta do better."

"Fuck that. Worry about it later. Now, I'm stuck, and I need you to come get me and change my tire! I'm like maybe twenty minutes from my house," I said, reminding him of my situation.

"I'm way out of pocket right now, so it would take me a while to reach you, but text me exactly where you at, and I'ma send Dom."

"No, don't send him," I whined. "He blocked my number and isn't speaking to me anyways, so I doubt he'll come."

"You're so damn dramatic. Y'all are not beefing, and he didn't block your shit. Trust me, I've been around him a few times when he's read your text. He's just teaching your spoiled ass a lesson. You can't always get what you want. I told you about playing with that man, but you didn't want to listen," he said.

"Spare me the lecture and just call him, Landon."

"That's what we on, huh? Okay, I'm about to call him with your big mad ass. Don't hang up. I'm calling him on my other cell phone," he said.

"Everybody ain't able," I said.

"I got two phones: one for the plug, and one for the load," his stupid ass said, singing Gates "Two Phones".

"Okay, keep on, and somebody gon' run off on the plug twice."

"Man, get the fuck on," he said, laughing. "But aye, I got Dom on my other line. He said hit his phone with your exact location.

"Tell him just find my phone on Where's My iPhone. He knows my iCloud information."

"Okay, he said he's on his way. Nigga sounded fucked up, so it's gon' be the blind leading the damn blind," he laughed.

"I guess he started his celebration already. I'll call you when he makes it."

"Shit, you're a fucking lie. You gon' stay on the phone with me until he makes it. I'll go crazy and kill every fucking thing breathing about you," his overprotective crazy ass said. Sad thing was he was serious as hell. We stayed on the phone just laughing and catching up until Dominic pulled up about thirty minutes later with the beat in his car slapping loud as hell.

"That gotta be his ass," Ghost said. "Loud ass speakers. He must've pulled out his old school tonight?" he asked, referring to Dom's 1977 ombré-colored Plymouth Cuda that was all souped up, from the huge rims he had on it to the new engine and motor he'd installed. I wasn't a fan of old-school cars, but I loved that car honestly, and he always looked so sexy when he pulled up in it.

"Yeah, you know that's the only thing that's that loud."

"Okay, well, hit me when you make it home. Love you."

"Love you more," I said, hanging up just as Dom cut the engine and got out the car, instantly making my panties wet as he walked his fine ass my way. Tonight, he was dressed simple but still was sexy in a fitted NY snapback, some gray sweatpants, a white Polo t-shirt, and jacket with fur on the hood. On his feet were a pair of fresh wheat Timberlands. My focus was on how that shirt was hugging every muscle on his body. Dominic was what women referred to as a big zaddy and seemed intimidating to some, but not me. I was so lost in lusting over him that I didn't even hear him knocking on my window.

Popping the locks to my car, he opened my door and said, "Damn, ma, you ain't hear a nigga knocking?"

"My bad," I said, biting my lip as my eyes traveled down his body to my best friend, whom I missed. It should've been a damn crime for men to wear gray sweatpants, like seriously, the shit should be illegal and hold a fine if caught wearing them, especially if he had a big dick. If it was small, then do not pass go, do not collect two hundred, go your ass straight to jail for that offense!

"You're funny as hell, bruh," he said, laughing because he must have realized I was raping him with my eyes. I finally looked into his face and noticed his eyes were bloodshot red. This nigga was higher than Snoop Dogg on 4/20.

"I'll pop the trunk. I got a spare in there."

"Well, come on 'cause a nigga ain't got all night." I got out the car and put an extra twist in my hips.

"Little ass poking out a bit back there," he said.

"Boy, bye." On the outside, I was very nonchalant as I walked to the trunk and popped it. But on the inside, I had my hands in the air and twerking, like 'aye, get it, bitch!'

"Boy, huh?"

"Yeah, boy, now can you please fix my tire so I can be on my way, and you can get back to fucking them raggedy hoes you ignore my texts for?" I asked, feeling very salty.

"Bet," he said, grabbing the tire and walking about to the passenger side.

"Damn, bruh, this shit busted as fuck. Ghost ugly ass said a flat—not a blown tire. You 'bout to have a nigga working, and I'm high as fuck right now," he said, walking back and grabbing my jack out of the trunk as well.

Shrugging my shoulders, I walked back to the driver side and grabbed my phone then came back to where he was so that I could cut my flashlight on and shine it where he could see. When he pulled off his jacket then took his off his shirt before he started, I damn near came all over myself. ‘

Get it together, bitch, I pep talked myself. The sexual energy between us was just too much. I hated it because, on the truthful tip, I hadn’t even been fucking with Mark like that. The last time I had sex with Mark, which was more than two month ago, I wasn’t into it at all, because I kept comparing the sex to Dom to the point I dried up like the Sahara Desert because Mark wasn’t whom my body craved. I would never tell Dominic’s ass this, though. I wasn’t about to let him think I was sitting around and waiting for him, shit.

It took him literally twenty minutes to change my tire.

“Thank you,” I said, getting into my car.

“I’ll follow you home. I need to wash up and take a piss anyway. Your place is closer,” he said as I noticed black oil marks all over his hands.

“Cool,” I said, starting my car up and pulling off onto the highway. We pulled up to my house at practically the same time, both of our asses hitting one hundred on the highway. My excuse was I was just ready to get home. I wasn't sure what his reasoning was. Getting out the car, I walked up to my door with him on my heels.

"Finally! I almost died," Tommie said as soon as I walked inside the house.

"Damn, bitch, I had a blowout. I really forgot to call you," I said to her, but I doubt she even heard me as she snatched the bags out my hand like a crackhead fiending for her next fix. "Well, damn."

"Thank you, Jas. Hey, Dom. Bye, Dom," she said, wobbling down the hallway toward her room.

"Her ass is something else," he said, laughing as he walked off toward the back of the house, I was guessing to the restroom. Grateful to be home, I went into my kitchen to grab myself some fruit to snack on out of the fridge with yogurt and a bottle of water. As I was walking out the kitchen and headed into my room, Dom and I crossed paths in the hallway.

"Make sure you lock the door on your way out!" I threw over my shoulder at him as I continued to my room. Walking inside, I sat the fruit down on my nightstand and popped a grape into my mouth as I opened my dresser drawers and grabbed some clothes out for my shower. Even though I had showered before I went to Walmart, I suddenly felt the need to take another one.

Turning some music on, I let Kelly Rowland's "Motivation" fill the room as I stripped out my clothes and walked into my bathroom, making sure to leave the door open so that I could hear the music. Stepping into my walk-in shower, I cut the water on and let it wash over me for a minute before I grabbed my Caress body wash and sponge, squeezing some onto it as I begin to rub it all over my body, and Kelly Rowland rang in my ear, saying *you can do it, I believe in you, baby.*

Oh, Lover, when you call my name

No other ... can do that the same, no

I won't let ya get up out the game, no

So go, lover, don't it make me rain

And when we're done, I don't wanna feel my legs

And when we're done, I just wanna feel your hands all over me, baby

Rocking my hips back and forth to the beat with my eyes closed, I imagined the shower doors opening. Eyes still closed, I really let the music take over me as I had the sponge on my body but had a slow grind going on at the same time. All into the music, I imagined that hands grabbed my hips, and someone was grinding into me as I started backing my ass up on them in a slow wind.

Normally, I could barely dance, but right now, I was fucking it up as I held the wall, bent over and throwing my ass like I was in a video. When I felt fingers creeping to the front of my body and invading my love nest, my eyes popped open because that shit felt real as hell. Quickly spinning around, I saw a very naked Dom standing there, eyes glazed over, looking at me like I was a snack.

"What-what are you doing in here?" I choked out as I tried not to allow my eyes to slide any further down than his face. Walking toward me, I started backing up until I felt my back hitting a wall, letting me know there was nowhere else to go. After all that shit I was talking, I was at a loss for words at this exact moment. Leaning down so that his mouth was level with my ear, he said, "I made sure to lock the door." Then, he licked my ear and down my neck. My body shuddered at his touch, and I swear, I felt like I came on myself. It had been so damn long since I'd felt his touch that I thought I would never be this intimate with him again.

"Am I dreaming?" I asked out loud.

Looking at me with those dreamy eyes that were hanging so low that they were damn near closed, he said, "Does this feel like a dream?"

"You said we were done and that you would never," I was saying but was silenced by his mouth crushing down onto mine. Taking that as my cue to stop talking, I relaxed and enjoyed the moment. I wasn't sure whether it was the fact that he was high or what that we were about to do this, but I wasn't complaining and planned to fully enjoy it.

Moving from kissing my mouth to kissing my breasts one at a time, that tantalizing tongue licked all over my stomach until he steadily descended lower. My body was on fire at this point, and my breathing had picked up as he spread both my legs apart and hungrily attacked my love nest like it was his last meal. Just as I was about to reach my peak, he suddenly stopped, stood up, and picked me up, wrapping my legs around his body.

Turning the shower off with one hand, he stepped out of the shower and walked over to my bed, gently placing me on top of my comforter, wet and all. Normally, I would have protested because this was a very expensive spread, but I felt like I was in a lust-induced state as I remained quiet, taking in everything that was happening. Walking over to his pants, he reached into his pockets and grabbed a condom and let the pants fall back to the ground. Walking back to me, he picked my legs up and pulled me to him as he ripped the condom open.

Still, I remained quiet as he rolled it onto his mushroom-shaped head and down his thick, long penis. The condom barely even went all the way down his dick, putting the myth about fat or big-muscled dudes having little dicks to rest. After securing the condom, I felt for sure he was about to invade my body with that magical wand that I had grown to love so much, but instead, he slowly climbed up my body and went back to his assault on my breasts.

Squirming around underneath him, I couldn't take this teasing much longer. I felt like I was going to explode, and I just wanted him to put this fire out that was brewing between my legs. Dom, however, must have had a different mission in mind as he took his time making love to each of my breasts before he finally reached his hand between our bodies. Knowing where this was headed, I thanked the Lord as I started gyrating my hips, bucking against him in eager anticipation of what was to come. When he stuck the tip in, I wrapped my legs around him, preparing to welcome both the pleasure I knew he would bring me as well as the pain that monster also delivered.

When I didn't feel him slide any further, I grabbed his ass, trying to push him further inside of me, but he quickly pulled out and went back to attaching my neck. Feeling myself about to lose my mind, I started shaking my head from side to side as I reached up and grabbed a handful of my hair. This fucking man was slowly making me go insane. I wanted to feel him inside of me so bad that I didn't know what to do.

Again, he reached his hands down and placed the tip in, and again, I bucked against the tip, trying to get him to slide further. My prayers were answered as he began sliding down into my love tunnel as I reached up and latched onto his juicy bottom lip, sucking on it as I prepared myself to go on the ride of my life. Just as I felt myself coming unglued, the wonderful feeling was snatched away from me as he once again pulled back out. I actually started crying as real tears began to slide down my face because I wanted him just that badly.

"Stop it, Dom," I cried.

"What you crying for?" he asked me, kissing my tears away. "Huh, Jasmine? What you crying for? Because you're not in control? Because you don't run shit? Because you don't listen to daddy, so I gotta punish you? That's why you're crying?" he asked me. Silent tears rolled down my face as I glared at him, pissed off and turned on at the same exact time. "Or are you crying because you want daddy to bless you with this big dick?" After I nodded my head, he continued.

"Is this what you want? Only obedient women get the dick. Are you obedient?"

Again, I nodded my head. Hell, I would agree to shave my head, empty my bank accounts, close all my social media, and change my name at this point. Hell, anything if it got me what I wanted.

"I don't believe you."

"Please, baby, I'm telling the truth, zaddy." I moaned as I squirmed under him. "Fuck this," I said. Reaching my hands down, I started playing with myself, but he quickly slapped my fingers away.

"So you not gon' fuck with that nigga no more?"

"No, I won't. I promise. I haven't even slept with him in almost two months!" I cried out. "You're doing this to me, but you're not even being faithful to me. You know what? I don't even want the dick anymore. Keep it."

At that exact moment, in one powerful thrust, he pushed inside of me roughly as he slid his entire eleven inches inside of me and immediately started pounding me hard, deep, and fast.

"What you don't want? Huh? What you don't want?" he asked in my ear, voice laced with passion as he delivered the best mind-blowing sex that we've ever had. Scooting up to get away from him because he was giving me every inch of him, he caught me around my waist and pulled me further down on his dick.

"Fuck! Ahh," I moaned. "You're so deep!" I cried out, putting my hand in between our bodies, trying to push him out a bit.

"Take this dick. It's yours. Take all of it. Fuck, my pussy's so tight and wet. Daddy the last one that was up in it, wasn't he?" he asked as he grabbed both my legs and put them across his shoulder, yet wanted me to answer him. All I could do was nod my head because I felt like my voice box was temporarily taken away from me.

"Fuck me back," he said as I started matching him stroke for stroke. Without warning, he pulled out of me and went down and started eating the soul out of my body. He was eating me so good that I felt my life flashing before my eyes as my soul left my body and went straight up to Heaven to chill with God. Ceasing his tongue assault, he flipped me over, and I didn't even have to be told to assume the position as I got on all fours and put that arch in my back.

"I got to feel this shit," he said as I heard the condom being pulled off. Once he went back in, I felt like he'd touched my spine as he grabbed me by the back of my throat with one hand and had a grip on my waist with the other hand so that I couldn't move anywhere or do anything other than take everything he was giving me.

"Fuck! Baby, oh my God!" I screamed. I was loud as hell, and I was sure Tommie and the entire block heard me, but at this point, I didn't even care. Hell, they would be loud too if they were getting the type of dick I was getting. Lying on my back, turning my head around to face him, he brought his mouth down on mine into a passionate kiss as he wrapped both arms around me and went even deeper inside me. Feeling his dick thumping and expanding, I knew he was close to nutting, and so was I from how he was hitting my G-spot and wouldn't let up off of it. Deepening the kiss, I started throwing my ass back on him as I felt the buildup in my stomach, and I knew that I was about to explode.

"I feel that shit, ma. Let it go. I'm right behind you," he said as he sped up his pace, reached around me, and played with my happy place. That was all it took as I let go of a mind-blowing, explosive orgasm.

"Oh, God, fuckkkk!" I screamed at the same time that Dom growled and emptied a football field of cum inside of me. I was too far gone to speak on the fact that he didn't pull out. I would just deal with that later. After he stopped shaking and cumming, he collapsed on my back as I fell flat on the bed. I didn't have the strength to move, to complain, or to do anything but fall fast asleep with a huge smile on my face, thinking *Mark who?* Hell, after sex like this, I had no plans of ever even talking to anybody with the initial M so that Dom wouldn't think I was checking for that nigga.

CHAPTER 7

RODNEY

"If this nigga ain't talking about shit, then we're getting up and leaving,".

"Man, fuck all that. You got the juice right now. What you need to keep doing is buying from Ghost, and just stacking your shit up so when y'all fall out again, you'll have something to fall back on," Mike said. He was beginning to piss me off lately with all this Ghost dick riding he was doing. Fuck that nigga Ghost with a sick dick. That nigga popped off on me about a bitch, and not just any bitch. My fucking bitch. I wasn't even mad about the situation anymore, but his ass wasn't fucking with a nigga like that anymore if it wasn't about business.

"Fuck Ghost," Monsta said to Mike, beating me to it. He and I had been rocking more lately, and besides being bat-shit crazy, the nigga was cool as hell.

"Shit, at least somebody's feeling me. But shit, I do agree on one thing. If this nigga's not talking about shit, then we do have to re-up from Ghost because the streets damn near dry right now, and niggas will move in on our territory quick if we don't make something shake," I said as we walked through the lobby of the hotel.

"It's some bad ass hoes in Houston," Monsta said as we got outside to pick the car up from the valet.

"Shit, yeah, my boy. I gotta snatch one up before we leave."

"Nigga, you was just talking about marrying Kelly," Mike's ass said. This nigga was blowing my high and starting to work my damn nerves.

"Shit, I agreed to be married. I didn't agree to give up my hoes."

"Look, Malcolm X, just because you back on good terms with yo' bitch don't mean the rest of us want to hear a damn lecture."

"This ain't about a bitch; this is about how you're fucking up everything we worked hard to build. You wasn't hugging the blocks by your damn self; I was right there beside you. Shit, you take shit too fucking far some damn times, and the only person you got to blame is your fucking self. You act like you're self-destructing or some shit. You talked all that shit about Tommie, but you're falling apart without her ass. You ain't been back to a hunnit since she did the dip. Yeah, you can put on a front all day for them niggas, but numbers don't lie. Shit, when you're playing with my money, yeah, I'ma speak on that shit. If you was any other nigga, I would have been came and saw about that shit. Y'all want to waste time and shit, chasing damn new connects when this nigga said he would still work with you, and that's being more than fair, considering the circumstances. Yeah, niggas do talk, so I know he's fucking with Tommie tough now. Word on the streets is that he's claiming that baby as well. Shit, instead of you bossing up and getting on your shit, you're doing this fucking stupid shit," Mike said to me.

This was the second time this nigga tried to check me on some fuck shit. I let that shit slide in the warehouse that day because maybe I was tripping, but this was strike two, and that nigga was in for a reality check if he thought shit was gon' be sweet after this. Niggas were sleeping on me, not realizing that was gon' cause them to get put to sleep permanently.

"I know my way. I'll meet y'all there," he said, brushing past me and walking off down the street.

"That nigga living on borrowed time," I said to Monsta.

"Shit, time I been waiting to snatch away. Say the word."

"Soon," I said as valet pulled up with our car, and we walked to get in so we could get to this meeting.

"Let's get this over with because time is money, and y'all done officially wasted about thirty unpaid minutes I can't get back. At least one of you had the decency to be on time," Midos said, looking annoyed with our asses the minute we walked in. Glancing around, I noticed the only people in the room were him and Mike, who looked like he had gotten a drink and gotten comfortable. The fact he didn't have any security made me feel like this nigga was a damn joke.

"Shit, my nigga, we had to find this piece of shit first. How you getting money and doing business meetings in some shit I wouldn't even push drugs out of?" I asked, looking at him like he was special or some shit. Getting a good look at him, I could tell he most definitely wasn't black; I just didn't know what he was mixed with.

"Because you're a clown ass nigga, and I didn't even take you serious to have this meeting in something fancy. See, I heard about the shit that popped off in the A, and I couldn't even believe you was still breathing. That's why I had to see the shit for myself. Let's not beat around the bush. Bottom line, yo' money not long enough to fuck with the big boys. Word is Ghost gives you double product at five thou a brick and only asks for half of the profit in return. You've been living the good life for years now. Shit, that's a steal, ole ungrateful ass nigga, because my shit's going for twenty-eight thou a brick, and if you want double product, them pockets better be doubled as well, and best believe, I need all my money and on time," he shot back, unfazed by me saying he couldn't have been getting money on big levels.

"Twenty-eight thousand a brick? What the fuck you smoking?"

"Nothing but the best. So like I said, when you ready to play with the big boys, then I'll take you seriously."

"Nigga, my money's good in any hood."

Laughing, he tossed a folder toward me as he got up from his chair, which happened to be the cleanest thing in this bitch.

Opening the folder, I was hit with my bank accounts, overseas accounts, and properties.

My shit was good as hell to me as I looked at the fruits of my labor. "What you giving me this for? Shit, my accounts say I can play with the big boys."

"What big boys you playing with? Your accounts say my hoes that I throw money to stand more of a chance of getting into business with me than your ass. Your spending is ridiculous, you can't manage your money to save your life, and you're a liability that I don't fucking need. Yeah, you have a few good businesses with okay profit, but Ghost was as good as it's gon' get for you. I'm saving both of us the hassle and bloodshed that will definitely occur if this shit was to go left because you decided to play with my money. I would hate to have to gas my G-5 up and make a trip to 225 Ausberry Lane and kill that mother of yours about my money, especially since she's been doing so good since the diabetes left. Would be such a shame if Kelly's pretty ass was to get tossed around by my niggas then fed to my dogs," he said, letting me know he knew every aspect of my life.

"But if this is what you want to do, then you better come correct," he said as he disappeared through a door, leaving us standing there, trying to process everything that had just happened.

"See," Monsta said, pointing in the direction that he just left. "Niggas like that—you don't need to fuck with."

"Daddy, let me tell you about me girlfriend," Karter said as I walked into the kitchen where he was sitting at the table while Kelly was making dinner. She had surprisingly taken to him better than I thought, which was a good thing for her ass because if she wouldn't have accepted him, I had a back-up bitch on standby who would have caught her slack. Kelly had been holding her own, though, even handling Amber's ass and all her Facebook drama without even breaking a sweat, which shocked me because she was so quiet when we first met. Shit, one day, Amber's ass approached us at Walmart, talking that rah-rah shit, but after Kelly told her ass that they could go outside to the parking lot and throw hands, her ass turned that gangsta all the way down.

"Boy, what girlfriend?"

"Me girlfriend, daddy. Ha name is Samantha," he said.

"Is she pretty?"

"Yeah, and she bought me some candy too, but ha booty was stanking today, so I don't know. We might be breaking up," the lil' nigga had the nerve to say. He even looked like the shit was stressing him out.

"Well, if she was stankin', you definitely need to break up with that hoe, son. She might try and give you something," I said, laughing.

Looking at Kelly, she just laughed, shaking her head as she brought plates to the table piled with food. She usually got on to me about talking to Karter like he was grown instead of four. Man, he was a smart ass four-year-old though because he really held conversations with me like he was much older. I'd be sitting down, running it to his ass all the time.

"Eat up. I'm about to go get cleaned," I said to him. Heading upstairs, I took a quick shower before I went to eat. I didn't even fully walk inside the room before Kelly came inside and closed the door. Thinking she wanted some dick, I walked closer to her only for her to put her hands up, pausing me.

"Who is Rachel?"

"Huh?" I asked, playing slow. I knew exactly who Rachel's fine ass was.

"Well, she wrote me on Facebook, saying she wanted me to know that our man got her pregnant."

"Man, that hoe ain't pregnant. Don't let her get to you."

"For her to be pregnant, you had to fuck her."

"I ain't touched that bitch. She's lying," I said, lying through my teeth because I did more than touch her ass.

"Let me see your phone."

"Fuck out of here, bruh," I said, walking past her to leave out the room.

"If you don't know her and have nothing to hide, let me see your phone."

I usually erased my phone before I came in the house, but I forgot to do that shit tonight. Fuck. Getting madder by the minute that I even had to come home and get questioned about this shit, I said, "I pay all the bills in this bitch, including my phone bill, so naw, you can't see shit unless you got the 145 for this month to pay this muthafucka," I told her.

When she walked off, I thought that was the end of the conversation until she came back with her purse and tossed two crisp one-hundred bills on the bed.

"There you go. Fuck you thought this was? Nigga, you asked me to move in with you—not the other way around—and I came in this relationship with my own shit. I wasn't a bum ass bitch you found in the hood and finessed. I can pay my weight my damn self. So again, since you threw out the number, there's two hundred, and you can keep the change, so let me see your phone," she said, throwing my ass for a complete loop. That shit usually worked with Tommie's ass, but Kelly was a little different. I see I was gon' have to break her ass down too and knock her off that high horse.

"You can't see shit," I said, walking closer to her, expecting her to back up toward the corner, but she didn't move an inch. Reaching my hands out with the intention of pushing her back, she reached out and kneed my ass in the balls.

"Nigga, I got three fucking brothers. Don't fucking try me like that."

"Wasn't nobody even about to hit your stupid ass," I said as I dropped to my knees and doubled over in pain. Of all the years I had been a dog ass nigga, it looked like I had finally met my match.

CHAPTER 8

DOMINIC

Pause, hold up, wait a minute. Oh shit, they done finally gave a nigga a chapter in the book, and y'all know I gotta show my ass. On the cool, I was salty as fuck about not getting a chapter in part one when I knew I was funnier than Ghost's ass, and I had more hoes than Rodney's ass, and I could fight better than Mike ass. Just hating on a real nigga, but it's cool. I'm here now, so it's up. Let me introduce my own damn self. I'm Dominic Reynolds, but don't ever call me that shit. It's Dom to you. Don't let Carmen get y'all fucked up calling a nigga by his government and shit. But shit, let's continue this book because I'm trying to get my fifteen minutes of fame and get discovered. I'm dropping all of my

Snapchat and Facebook information after this, so hit a nigga up, though.

Leaving from Jasmine's house, I stopped at Chipotle because I was hungry as hell. I had a taste for one of those damn fire ass steak bowls this early in the morning. Whipping into a parking spot, I cut my engine and got out, heading toward the door. I made it to the entrance at the same time as this cute female, so doing the gentlemanly thing, I opened the door for her.

"Thank you," she said as she walked ahead of me inside the building, allowing me to catch a glimpse of her ass jiggling like Jell-O in the scrubs she had on. Trying to be on my best behavior because I had just left Jas's house, I contained myself, so picked up my phone to check my messages, trying to busy myself with anything just so I wouldn't get in trouble. As crazy as she came off, Jasmine was right. You got out what you gave into a situation, and I wanted all of her—mind, body, and soul—so I was going to try this thing called monogamy. Hopefully this go-around, it would be better than in the past

"I'm sorry. I couldn't help but notice your car when I was walking in. I love old-school classic cars. I myself have an old-school Camaro my dad gave me," big booty Judy said as she turned around to me.

"Word? What year?" I asked her because I collected old-school cars like clothes and would buy it off her pretty ass if it was nice.

"It's a 1968 Camaro RS with a rebuilt engine and motor custom built by my dad. He loved that car, and before you ask, no, sir, it's not for sale," she said, looking down at her phone while she was talking. When she looked up, she was holding her phone up to my face. I almost got angry at the fact that her fingers were practically touching me until I realized she was showing me a picture of the car. Looking closely at it, I immediately fell in love. That shit was so damn clean; I had to cop me one.

"Where'd he get that from?" I asked her.

"It was his first car."

"That's dope," I said, admiring the fact she was a lover of older models as well. Curious to know if they sold them at the auction, I pulled up google and began searching for one as I noticed out the corner of my eye people moving up in line. Walking forward with my head still in my phone without looking, I accidentally bumped into the softest thing next to cotton that I'd ever felt. *Down, boy.*

"I'm sorry," I said.

"No, that's okay. It happens. I mean people bump into me all the time, merely that accidents happen. By the way, I'm Morgan," she replied, offering me a warm, welcoming smile and extending her hand out for me to shake.

"My apologies, but I don't really do handshakes. People don't wash their hands and shit, and you got scrubs on, so for all I know, you work with all them people changing dirty diapers and cleaning up shit," I said truthfully.

"Actually, I work at a hospital."

"That's even worse, but I'm Dom. Sup," I said, hitting her ass with a head nod. I was serious about that handshake thing. It had nothing to do with me not wanting to make skin contact with her sexy ass. Hell, she could be sexy and dirty for all I knew. After I ordered my food, I hopped in my car and headed to the one place I loved more than this car: my house.

Getting on the highway, I couldn't help but let my mind drift to Jasmine and what went down last night—well, technically, this morning. I really only came to help her with her flat tire, and that was it. It was my intentions to simply fix the tire, go to her place, get cleaned up, and leave. I didn't plan on everything that went down, but after I saw her, it was just hard to resist. Shit, it had been hard for me to keep my hands off her since I finally got her lil' chocolate ass.

I'd been checking for Jas since I first laid eyes on her a few years ago. She was the smartest, coolest, most down to earth chick I'd ever met. She didn't judge a nigga by what was in my pockets, and my clout in these streets didn't faze her one bit. She genuinely liked me as a person, not because of what I could do for her. When we linked up, we always had fun together, from hopping on the Xbox together, hitting a movie, or just Netflix and chill.

I felt like, with her, I could be myself and not have to be this hard ass monster all the time. We talked about any and everything, and she'd never judged a nigga off my past and was always listening to what I had to say and even responding with solid advice. I even told her about my past relationship that damn near broke me mentally—hell, only Ghost and Pops knew that story up 'til that point.

Shit, it was my fuck ups that landed us in the current situation we were in. Me thinking with my dick and not my head. She'd walked in on my dicking this bitch Toya down properly, and ever since then, she said she was cool with us doing our own thing on the side. Hell, I didn't know why I did it, because couldn't nobody's pussy in the past compare to her shit.

Truthfully, I was jealous of her square ass doctor nigga. She had something in common with him that she didn't have with me, and I felt like he was a better choice for her. I barely got my GED. Tonight was so special because of the fact I'd finally passed this business course Ghost had me going to. Not only did I have my associates in business, I also now had my license. All the other businesses Ghost had said were both of ours—because he was a real ass nigga like that—were legally only his, but he still gave me my cut from them, though. However, Fly Guys was both of ours and my pride and joy. Not bad for a nigga from the hood who grew up in a trap house with no lights half the time.

Ring, ring!

Looking down at my phone, I noticed it was Ghost calling me. Turning onto my street, I answered the phone as I pulled up to my gate. Entering the code, the steel gates swung open, revealing a long, circular driveway. You would assume—being that I purchased this home for my ex fiancé, and now that it was just me—I would rarely sleep here. That wasn't the case at all. Shit, I worked hard for this five-bedroom, four-and-a-half bathroom, five thousand square feet, Contemporary-style home, and I loved coming home to peace and quiet.

"Hello?"

"Damn, nigga, I've been calling your ass all night. Where you at?"

"Just pulling up to my house."

"Shit, I'm not even going to ask where yo' ass been because Jas wasn't answering her phone either, and I told her wobble head ass to call me when she made it."

"Whatever, my nigga," I said, turning my car off and getting out.

"All that shit you was talking about fuck her, and you was done, ole soft ass nigga. Lil' sis got yo' ass whipped like pancake batter. I should have took a bet out."

Laughing, I said, "I know yo' ass not talking. Tommie ass got you whipped worse than a fat kid addicted to Lil' Debbie cakes. Nigga, that's why you text her ass instead of seeing her, so fuck you, ole ugly ass nigga. Ain't even tasted the pussy and buying cars and shit," I said, referring to the tricked out 2017 Audi truck he bought her as a push gift that he planned on giving to her when she had the baby. Nigga ain't never even heard of that shit, but he said he saw it on Instagram that women got push gifts, so he insisted on getting her a car.

"That's where you're always going wrong at, minding my business bitch, and I did taste the pussy, so fuck you. Anyway, did set that rat trap like I asked?" he asked, referring to the trap we set for whomever the rat in our camp was. We leaked false drop locations and fake names and only told a select few then leaked some more and told another few, so when and if it got back to us, we would know exactly who the snitch was.

"Yeah, I set that shit. But check it, I knew I had to tell you something yesterday. I was just high as fuck and forgot."

"What?" he asked.

Opening up my fridge, I grabbed some bread so I could whip up a sandwich to hold me over until I ate tonight.

"How 'bout Rodney's ass sent in his money for the month and requested another drop."

"Okay," Ghost said, and I had to pull the phone away to make sure I was hearing right. My ass couldn't have still been high from last night.

"What you mean okay?"

"Nigga, I beat the nigga's ass and made sure he felt me when I said he wasn't to come near my fucking child. Other than that, I don't got no beef with him like that. I ain't fucking with him heavy like I used to, but that's still family, and I'm his connect. This is business, not personal. We ain't having get togethers no more or no shit like that, and if he looks wrong at Tommie or Royalty, that nigga's dead. As long as he plays his part, we're good. He can re-up."

"My nigga, is you serious right now? I don't trust that snake ass nigga, bruh. He's out here living foul, and if the nigga didn't live in Atlanta and didn't know about half the people names that was on that list Kelina gave us, I would have bet my life on it that his bitch ass was behind this."

"Shit, I thought that as well but remembered that way before I found out Tommie was his baby's moms, I was in Houston, tracking down Henry's folks and shit, so it can't be him. We ain't have no smoke before now."

"Man, fuck that. I don't trust his ass."

"Shit, me either, but until he crosses me, I'ma rock with his ass. I ain't beefing about no female that thinks I'm a foul ass nigga anyway."

"Whatever. You can talk that rah-rah shit to a nigga who don't know yo' lil' dirty ass personally, but not the nigga who's been knowing you."

"Fuck you, nigga. We still linking up before the event, or you just gon' meet me there?"

"Naw, I'll meet your ass there because Kelina's Roger Rabbit looking ass acts like she can't leave your side for a few minutes, and I don't like that broad, bruh. It's something suspect about her ass, too."

"You're one paranoid ass nigga, you know that? Now she's suspect too?" he asked, laughing. "I'll get up with you later, but aye, I'm proud of you. You know that, right?"

"Yeah, I know," I said, hanging up as I walked upstairs, heading to the master bedroom. When I hired an interior designer to decorate it, I wanted to do something different from the usual black and gold themed rooms I always saw on those home-makeover channels. On the outside, I was a simple nigga. I wasn't flashy at all, but everything I had on cost money.

However, I spared no expense when it came to my house, from the eight thousand Villa Valencia king-size poster canopy bed that made a nigga feel all presidential and shit. It cost me another two racks to add black lights to it and a mirror on top of my canopy so that when I was hitting my future wife from the back, I could look up at myself. So far, the only person that had ever been in that bed was Jas, so I guess that should tell me something. The custom-made space-gray Eliasa Ecru Winter Grade A Iceland Eiderdown oversized comforter set complete with dark gray, charcoal gray, white, and black decorative pillows set me back twelve hundred, but it set my entire bedroom set off. On my wall were two huge pictures of Scarface and other black and white pictures of Tony Montana that faced either wall. A gray chaise sat directly in front of my bed along with a black and gray rug on the side of the bed to the right of it.

Walking to my huge walk-in closet that had a couch, a bar, and bathroom inside, I walked over to make myself and drink and took a seat to decide exactly what I wanted to wear. I figured I would trade my sweatpants and jeans in for some slacks and a button down. A nigga could go GQ magazine when he wanted to. Once I got my clothes together, I went back inside my room and laid across my comforter, pressing a button on my headboard, and a sixty-five-inch HD smart TV slid down from the ceiling.

I told you; I spared no expense when it came to my house. Shit, a nigga never had shit, so I was gon' sit back and enjoy the fruits of my hard labor. Flipping through channels, I stopped on ESPN and decided to catch up with the highlights of the week. An hour into watching, I got to thinking about Jasmine, so I decided to text her to see if she'd gotten up from her coma-induced sleep yet because she usually slept all day after I beat the pussy up.

You up shawty?

As I was pressing send on the message, I accidentally pressed answer on my phone, which happened to be ringing at the exact same time. *Fuck, I was not trying answer this bitch's call.*

"Dom? Dom?" she said.

"What you want, Jackie?"

"Please, I need you. I didn't know who else to call." Rolling my eyes to the ceiling, I said, "You never know who else to fucking call. Look, get off my phone line. I told your junkie ass don't fucking call me."

"Please, I just need your help. I-I-he won't let me leave. I'm tired of this, Dom. I want to get clean for my daughter, but I don't know how."

"Daughter?" I whispered. Jackie was once the love of my life and was pregnant with my child when she overdosed on the very drug I was flooding the streets with. Shit fucked me up.

That was why I had this house built from the ground up—because I thought I was getting the family I never had. That was when I went to Ghost and told him we had to start making moves on a bigger level, and literally overnight, his pops' best friend handed him the crown, and thus, our empire took off.

My vision was to have everything done by the time my baby got here. However, that vision never turned into my reality after that bitch overdosed and almost died, which resulted in her pushing out a dead baby into this world. The doctors said if my baby had lived, then she would have lived a life of pain because she possibly would have had so many different complications and problems due to the excessive drug misuse. That was actually the only reason Jackie lived because her body didn't have as many drugs in it as her child's. When she lost my child, there was no coming back from that for that hoe. I had been on some 'fuck hoes get money' type shit ever since then. That was almost five years ago.

"Yes, I have a three-year-old daughter."

"Funny how you cared enough not to overdose with her like you did our daughter."

"Please, Dom, I just need you to come get us. It doesn't matter where you take us; we just have to get away from here before he turns to my baby. I regret everyday what I did to our daughter. I wasn't well, and I had problems you couldn't even begin to image, but I want to be okay for my daughter now. The Lord gave me a second chance to be a mother."

"And you repay him by still getting high? He needs to stop saving your ass," I said, still very much angry with her ass now as I was when I kicked her out of my life.

"I don't willingly use, Dom. When I don't do what Kenneth wants, he holds me down and sticks me with a needle. I'm a prisoner in my own home, and I just want to do better for my daughter. She'll be four soon," she said, further hurting me by revealing that not only did she kill my baby, but less than a year later, she was pregnant again. So she must've been cheating on me all along.

"So you was unhappy with me, a nigga who only tried to love you and wanted a family, yet you have a baby by a nigga that's beating your ass?"

"He's never hit me before."

"Shit, you said he forces you to take drugs, so if he doesn't hit you, how is he forcing you to take drugs?" I asked because I was confused at this point and annoyed as hell with the conversation.

"Okay, so he doesn't hold me down and force me, but he buys the shit and bribes me to do things I don't want to do and gives it to me as a reward. I always feel so dirty afterward," she said as she started to cry. "Look, never mind. Forget I ever called."

"Send me the address," I said, checking the time to see that it was still only two in the afternoon and early. I was only going for the child—not her ass. I didn't give a fuck if that bitch lived or died, but it sounded like they had some damn crack hoe house going on, and I didn't want the baby to be part of that shit.

"Thank you for doing this for me, I really appreciate it. I promise—"

Cutting her off, I said, "I didn't do shit for you, and if you were solo, yo' ass would be still bussing it wide open for that crack. I'm doing this for that baby," I said as I heard a ding on my phone, indicating she had sent the address. She grew silent for a second, probably absorbing in what I said.

"I snuck and used the phone because this was my only chance, so I won't be able to answer when you call, but I promise I will be ready," she said as the line went dead. *What the hell did she mean by that shit?* I wondered as I got up and went back into my walk-in closet, pressing a button that flipped over to reveal my gun collection. Grabbing my baby—a chromed-out desert eagle—I tucked it into the back of pants just in case I had to show these fools who not to play with and walked out the closet and out the room. When I got to my car, I hopped in and pulled up my text messages so that I could input the address into my GPS system. Before I pulled off, I checked to see if Jas had texted me back, which she hadn't, but it showed that she read my text. Shaking my head at females and their mixed signs and emotions, I drove out of my driveway, headed to my destination with thoughts of what Jasmine was doing that she couldn't text me back on my brain.

CHAPTER 9

GHOST

I was starting to feel like I kept hitting dead ends after dead ends as I searched for answers on who killed Henry and who the mole in my camp was. The only thing I was accomplishing was a pile of bodies in my wake. Niggas were slowly reawakening a beast that wasn't anything nice. I was gon' get to the bottom of this shit if it was the last thing that I did.

Glancing at the clock, I noticed it was nearing nine a.m., and I had yet to go home and wash my ass and rest up for the grand opening of our new store later on tonight. Following this lead on Henry's killer led me to this cat named Shun, who apparently was the nigga to see for answers. Well, that was what the last nigga told me before I put a bullet in his head, so if this nigga didn't know shit, then he was meeting the same fate as well.

Posted up outside his house, I planned on paying him a friendly house call whenever he decided to make his way home. Waiting for him, I texted Tommie, telling her to tell my daughter good morning and that Daddy loves her. I honestly didn't know what fate held for her and me, but my daughter would never have to doubt nor question my love. Four hours later, I decided to give up for now, but rest assured that Shun would be getting another visit soon. Cranking up my busted down '98 Acura, I drove to my condo with the intentions on showering and falling straight into my bed, not waking up until I had to for tonight.

"Fuck." I moaned as Kelina swallowed half of my dick effortlessly without choking once, causing my eyes to pop up, looking down as my dick repeatedly hit the back of her throat.

"This big dick tastes so good," she said as she started French kissing my shit, literally making love to it with her mouth. I felt as if I were in heaven as she skillfully spat on my dick and took me back down her throat. Her gag reflexes were on point as she, with skill, deep throated my dick like it nothing. This was, by far, some of the best head I'd ever had in my entire life. Wrapping my hands tightly in her hair, I attempted to shove more of my dick into her mouth when she quickly jerked back like I had burned her or some shit.

"What the hell, Ghost? You know how I feel about that!" she said, and I already knew what she was referring to.

"Well, if you don't want me pulling the shit, keep it in a ponytail," I said as I felt my erection deflating while listening to the bullshit she was spitting. Kelina and I had grown closer these last two months, and she was somewhat my girl but not really because I wasn't ready to fully commit to her just yet. It was something in my gut holding me back, and I always trusted my gut. I kept telling her we weren't official, but I doubted she was hearing me, but I was still sure to remind her when she acted like she forgot or got on that jealous shit.

"I don't have a problem with you pulling it; you're just always pulling my hair so damn tight. Hell, last time, you pulled an entire track down, and that was a fresh sew in."

"Nobody told you to wear the shit," I mumbled as my dick went fully limp at this point. Moving her to the side, I got off the bed ass naked with the intentions of going to take a shower so that I could start getting dressed.

"Are you mad?" she asked me as I completely ignored her ass.

"Naw, I'm good."

"But you didn't let me finish. I'm sorry, you can pull it."

"I said I was good, so drop it and get dressed. You know it takes your ass a long time to get ready," I said to her, but she didn't accept my answer because she pushed me back onto the bed and wrapped her juicy lips around my now limp dick. I tried to push her head away, but my dick had a mind of its own as it sprang back to life. Licking and slobbering all over my shit, she started going to town as she jerked me and sucked me at the same time. Pulling my dick out of her mouth, she hit my dick against the side of her face a few times before she lifted up and sucked both of my balls gently into her mouth.

I almost lost it right then and there. Releasing my balls and placing my dick back into her mouth, she began sucking on my shit like she was playing football and was in the fourth quarter, racing against the clock as she went into overdrive. As a habit of mine that was hard to break, my hands had a mind of their own as they found their way into her hair, getting a good grip as I began fucking her face like I would if I were beating that pussy up.

Feeling myself reaching my peak, I said, "Fuck, I'm about to nut. Catch this shit, girl," as I busted a huge nut inside her mouth seconds later. Like the true freak that she was, she took it all in and continued sucking until she had gotten everything out of me that she could. Releasing my dick, she opened her mouth, showing me my kids, before swallowing everything down with a smile.

"Freaky ass."

"Only for my man," she said, getting up and walking into the bathroom as I gave her a blank stare. A few seconds later, I heard water running, followed by her gurgling what I assumed to be mouthwash. Coming back out of the bathroom, I was still giving her a crazy look.

"What?" she asked, wiping her face with a towel.

"What I tell you about that man shit?"

"What you mean, Ghost? I'm always at your house, I don't see another bitch popping up, you always be sure to make it home for dinner sometimes, we do shit like a couple, and you fuck me really good like I'm your girlfriend. Shit, what else are we then?"

"We're cooling, bruh. We both know what is it—no need to try and complicate shit," I said, getting up for the second time and, this time, making it to the bathroom. That nut was exactly what a nigga needed to get me through this night. That and a blunt because my nerves were on edge. I couldn't explain it, but I had a bad feeling like something was gon' jump off. Whatever the case was, I was gon' be prepared for whatever.

"So you saying I can give this pussy to whomever?" Kelina asked me as soon as I walked into the room from the shower.

"Shit, if that's what you want to do." I shrugged because I honestly didn't have a say in what she did. I probably wouldn't be knocking her off if she did, though. Contrary to the perception women had of men, not all of us were fucking multiple people at once. I'd been there, done that, and the shit didn't excite me anymore. She was the only person I was sleeping with at the moment, but of course, telling her that wouldn't be wise. She would either take that as we really were together, or I was lying on my dick and was really fucking anything over eighteen with a pussy.

"So you don't care? Really, Ghost?" she asked, slicing through my thoughts, making me refocus on her. I had tuned her out and hoped she'd get the hint and stop talking.

"Look, Kelina, I like you and think you're a cool girl. Maybe if you chilled out and played your part, we could be more, but you be doing too much, ma. Shit, you started out laid back and chill; now you're this crazy, nagging ass person who I can't get to leave my side for five minutes out the day without a complaint."

"Quit fucking me so good then," she said, shrugging like that was the solution to our problem.

"I don't know how to deliver weak dick, but even if I cut back, that wouldn't fix shit."

"It could be a start."

Shaking my head, I continued looking through my drawers for a specific tie, only to realize I'd left it at home. I was currently at my condo because the only person who had the privilege to lay their head where I laid mine, was Tommie.

"Listen, shawty, I gotta run home and finish getting dressed, but when I get back, I need you dressed and ready to go."

"And that's another thing. When am I going to ever be allowed to come to your actual home? You got me tucked away like a side bitch."

"You actually brought your clothes here and just never left," I said, interrupting her. She didn't say anything; she just shot me an evil look. I wasn't even trying to be funny. I was merely stating facts. Shit, I didn't bring her ass anywhere. She drove herself one night when I invited her over and came back each night after that until she just stopped leaving altogether. She looked sexy as hell when she was mad with her chest heaving up and down rapidly. Walking over to her, I picked her up and sat her on top of the dresser.

"Why you giving daddy a hard time, ma?" I asked her as I started sucking on her neck at the same time as my hands found the inside of her shorts, and my fingers invaded her dripping pussy. I knew this was all she wanted. She wasn't fooling anybody with that tantrum she was throwing.

"Ahh." She moaned, throwing her head back in pure bliss.

"This what you wanted, huh?" I asked her as I inserted another finger inside her. Grabbing her by her throat and gently squeezing it, applying pressure but not enough to hurt her, I licked her from her chin up to her mouth as my fingers moved in and out of her at a rapid pace as if it were my dick.

"You gon' stop tripping on a nigga?" I asked her.

"Oh my God, yes!" she replied. I wasn't sure whether she was saying yes to my question or the fact I'd added yet another finger inside of her, heightening my assault on that pussy. My whole hand was soaked, and a puddle was forming on the floor as she bucked against my fingers, wrapping her legs around my body, making me push deeper inside of her.

"Mmhh, baby!" She moaned as her eyes were rolling in the back of her head. Leaning forward and sucking her nipple through her shirt really pushed her over the edge as she lost it and started creaming all over my arm and lower stomach. I let her have her moment and allowed her to come down off her high before I asked, "You good now?"

"Yes," she said, nodding her head rapidly up and down.

"Good, now go get cleaned up and ready because when I get back in an hour, I expect you dressed and walking out the door when I pull up. Understood?"

"Hell yeah, I understand," she said, smiling. Her whole demeanor had changed just that fast. She now had a glow about her, and that nasty attitude was gone. Releasing her, I walked into the bathroom to clean myself up so that I could go home and get dressed. Once I was dressed and out to my car, I started to wonder if I was doing to Kelina what Tommie had done to me by not giving her a fair chance because of someone else's mistake? Deciding I would at least try, I headed home.

The grand opening celebration was in full swing by the time Kelina and I showed up. We looked good as hell if I do say so myself, especially her. She matched my fly perfectly in her black Valentino dress that hugged every natural curve on her body. That shit was fitting her like a second skin, and I had a mind to duck off in one of these rooms and give her ass the business. Stopping to pose for the cameras, we then made our way inside the store. I hadn't seen it since they finished with the renovations, and I must say they outdid themselves with this three-level clothing store that also had a Starbucks and snack bar inside.

"I see some people I know, so I'm going to go mingle. Besides, here comes Dominic, and I don't want to be bothered with him tonight," she said, rolling her eyes as Dom was approaching us. She didn't like him, and the nigga hated her ass, but I think it was just because he was team Tommie all the way, but shit, she'd pushed me away. I didn't get rid of her.

"My nigga," Dom said, walking up to me, dapping me up.

"Enjoy yourself, baby," Kelina said, giving me a kiss before walking off.

"I don't even know why you brought that hoe," Dom said with his face all turned up.

"Not tonight," I said, not in the mood to hear about his dislike for her or her snake ways, which I had yet to see for myself because if I did, I would personally kill the bitch myself.

"You're right," he said, adjusting his tie.

"Nigga's out in the bitch casket sharp," I said, laughing and referring to his attire. It wasn't unusual for me to switch it up from business attire to street clothes, but this nigga wouldn't be caught dead in anything other than street clothes. Shit, I barely recognized the nigga tonight. This was really more his night than mine, though, so I guess that was why he dressed the part. He was the one responsible for doing everything from securing the payments to overseeing the design to the layout. This was his vision, not mine. I merely supplied the permits. I already had my stores.

However, since I'd made him silent partner in all my ventures, he wanted this to be ours as well. A person could never understand our relationship and how much of a real nigga both of us were. Glancing toward the entrance, I saw Tommie and Jasmine walking in, headed toward us. It was like everything and everybody disappeared as my eyes zeroed in on Tommie, looking angelic and glowing. It had been two months since I physically saw her even though I made sure to text her every night. She was so damn sexy and beautiful, even with her stomach big as hell. It seemed as if she floated over to me as she grew closer and closer. Her perfume invaded my nostrils before she even fully reached me.

"Nigga, you're staring at that girl like you want to sop her up like a piece of biscuit and gravy," Dom said.

"Man, ain't nobody checking for her ass," I lied, but I couldn't stop the smile from forming on my face.

Once they reached us, Jasmine was the first to speak, reaching out and hugging me.

"Congrats, brother. I love you, and I'm so very proud of you," she said.

"Congrats, Landon. This is another major accomplishment for you. I wish you nothing but great success moving forward. Big congratulations are in order for you as well, Dom," Tommie said, hugging Dom as best she could, given her huge, protruding belly. When I didn't get a hug as well, I felt a twinge of jealousy, which I didn't know why, because just the other day, I was adamant about not wanting her, and just a few hours ago, I was sure I'd give Kelina a fighting chance.

"Thank you, ma. At least somebody acknowledged me tonight," he said, cutting his eyes at Jasmine.

"Oh, hey, Dom. I didn't even see you standing there."

"But you saw this dick this morning when it was repeatedly hitting them guts," he shot back.

"Whoa, language. I accepted the fact my sister having sex. Shit, I don't want to hear about her sex life."

"Man, fuck her ass," he said.

"Fuck you, nigga. You dipped on me to go be with another bitch then didn't have the decency to call."

"You sound as stupid as you look. I left to come get situated for my big night, and I did text your ass."

"Yeah, texted me, but you didn't call, so that means I wasn't even worth a call, so fuck you. I know a nigga who thinks I'm worth the world."

"Man, I'm done with you for good," Dom said to her.

"Shit, that's fine because I was done with your ass for good the minute you left, so done. I need to go to Atlanta and get properly dicked down," she said grabbing, Tommie by the arm and dragging her off into the crowd. With her eyes, Tommie silently apologized to me for the shit that just jumped off.

"Nigga, what the fuck just happened?" I asked him

"I left her sleep to go to the house, get my mind right, and chill out. I wanted to take the time to reevaluate where we were going, and I had decided to give this relationship thing a shot and wanted her to be my date tonight. I don't need this shit right now. Some mad shit already jumped off that had a nigga really on another level anyway," he said.

Immediately becoming concerned, the smile I was wearing a few seconds ago quickly left my face.

"It's about the rat? Somebody bit the cheese?" I asked, speaking in code, referring to the fake information we had put out.

"Naw, shit, I wish so that we could go kill their asses and get the shit over with. I'm sick of having to move like we've been doing even though it's smarter. Shit, this was the purpose of bossing up, elevating our status, and hiring a team, paying them to do all this shit. Got a nigga working like a runaway slave or some shit. Making drops and picks ups myself in this below-freezing weather all day. I know I'ma turn into a snowman in a minute."

"Bruh, you're always overplaying shit. Just turn your heater on, and you'll be okay."

"Shit, not when it's colder than Alaska on a sunny day. But, umm, the situation I ran into was Jackie."

"Jackie? Crackhead Jackie?" I asked in disbelief because I was sure she would have smoked her knee caps off by now. "Shit, she's still looking like Wanda from *Holiday Heart*? I got the bike," I said, imitating her family scene where she had the bicycle but got hit by the car in the process.

"Chill out. She's in recovery," he said, laughing. A waiter came over with wine glasses, and I sent his ass away to get the Hennessy Black that I had chilling on ice specifically for us. Fuck I look like drinking some damn wine?

"Can we get a photo with you two together?" one of the photographers asked, walking up to us."

"Yeah," I said as Dom and I struck a player-made pose.

After he left, Dom said, “Shit, let’s go do some meet and greets and work the crowd.”

“Bet, but, nigga, don’t think I forgot about that shit either.” Walking off, I spoke to a ton of people and posed for countless pictures.

“Baby, there you are,” Kelina said, walking up to me. Baby girl was truly wearing the hell out of that dress. Grabbing her by the waist, I pulled in for a juicy kiss as I heard camera flashes.

“You look beautiful, you know that?”

“Yes, because you told me,” she said, smiling brightly, and she reached up to adjust my tie. “You hungry, baby?”

“Yeah, go fix me a plate,” I told her, and she walked off to the area where we had the food. Walking over to Jasmine’s mom, I shot her a fake smile as I gave her a hug. I couldn’t stand this woman, but I tolerated her off the strength of her husband.

“How are you?” she asked me all tight lipped.

“I’m cool,” I said, keeping it short and brief.

“I see you took my advice and got rid of that girl and all her problems. Maybe now she can go bother her actual baby’s father if she even knows who that is. Like mother like daughter," she said. I had to count backward to keep myself from snatching her old ass up.

"She doesn't have to find shit, because she knows who her child's father is, and it's me. Worry about your marriage before Pops leaves your ass for a young bitch that I'll throw him on," I said, brushing past her ass. I wasn't going to let her even fuck up my night tonight.

A few hours later, and the party was finally winding down, and majority of everyone had gone home, and mostly my crew and a few scattered folks remained. We had surprisingly had quite a turn out, and everything went very smoothly. So much for that gut feeling I had been having all night. Maybe a nigga had to shit or something.

"Kelina, come on so I can introduce you to my baby momma."

"Why?"

"I figured if you were going to be in my life and maybe a part of my child life, then you needed to meet her mother."

"Can I take a rain check on that?" she asked, and I could have sworn I detected a hint of attitude.

"Yeah, it's late anyway."

"I'm going to go to the restroom," she said, walking off as she pulled out her phone to text somebody, not even bothering to wait for my reply.

"What the hell was all that about?" Dom asked, walking up just as she was walking off.

"Shit, I don't know, but I'ma find out later. But nigga, I haven't forgot. What's recovery? And how you know Jackie's not running game on yo' sucker for love ass?" I asked him as I put my glass to my mouth. I was taking a sip when this nigga said something that had me damn near choking to death.

"She has a daughter, and they're both at my house, so I know she's at least trying to get clean."

I started checking his head to make sure he was okay as he swatted my hands away.

"Gon' on with that gay shit."

"Fuck you. I was trying to check to make sure yo' ass wasn't sick because surely you can't be in your right mind to leave a crackhead at your house. Please tell me you ain't take her to your real home—as in the one you built for her. I know you took her to the condo."

When he didn't respond, I really felt like I needed to go have another smoke break.

"Bruh, I got this, okay? It was a spur of the moment thing. I had just gotten them from this hoe house and—"

"Hoe house? So she's selling ass now?" I asked because I had to hear this shit.

"Hey, sons," OG Menace said, walking to me. Shit, I hadn't seen his ass all night.

"I thought you didn't make it," Dom said.

"Sup," I said, dapping him up and pulling him into a hug. I loved this man to death, and he was the closest thing I had to a father. Being that he and my father were best friends, I always felt connected to my father through the stories Menace would tell me. We talked more than most people spoke to their own parents. Hell, I knew we talked more than him and Jas. He schooled me on the game and gave me great life lessons.

"What y'all lil' niggas over here talking about? Y'all been huddled up so damn long."

"Shit, I was just saying how we needed to get you some new pussy," I told him. He knew I couldn't stand his wife. Shit, I wondered, at times, if even he could stand the bitch himself.

"Hell yeah," Dom said, laughing.

"My pimp hand been strong. Y'all can't get me shit when y'all can barely get y'all selves anything. Still wet behind the ears and shit," he shot back.

Laughing, I said, "Pops, this nigga done left crackhead Jackie at his house."

"Same one who overdosed and killed the baby?" he asked for clarity.

"Yes."

"Damn, can y'all stop saying crackhead Jackie?" Dom asked.

"Son, that could be a dangerous situation. Drugs are a powerful thing to shake. It will make even the most strong-willed person act out of character. She could very well be setting you up to be robbed or, worse, you could come home and everything be gone."

"Pops, it's not even like that. She called me to get away from this pimp ass nigga, and I only helped her out because of her daughter. You know I don't care if that hoe lives or dies."

"How you know it's her baby and not just a fucking lie she told? She could have kidnapped that baby and pretended like it was hers because she knows you wouldn't turn her away with a kid. Shit, do the baby even look like her?" I asked him.

"Now you're thinking. You always have to stay one step above these hoes," Menace said.

Dom was getting ready to respond when, out of nowhere, shots rang out. Ducking down, we each drew our gun at the same time and began bussing back at the intruders. My crew ran out from around the corner and up the stairs, all firing their guns in the directions that the bullets were flying from.

"Who the fuck these niggas is?" Dom asked as we ran to the other side of the store where our niggas were.

"Shit, I don't know, but I have to make sure Tommie okay," I said, looking frantically around for her. She was the first and only person that popped in my head.

"Kill everything moving!" Pops yelled, and my men took off toward whoever was firing. We couldn't see anybody, but we for damn sure saw the bullets. Being high up on the balcony or something, they had an advantage over us, but we weren't backing down for shit.

Running around the store like I was invincible as I searched for Tommie, not giving a fuck about the bullets flying. Hearing commotion to my left, I pointed my gun in that direction. I was about to light that bitch like a firecracker when Kelina suddenly appeared, running full speed toward me.

"Thank God it's you, Ghost. I heard gunshots and got scared and came over here," she said, looking around. The paranoia in me was looking at her suspect as she looked around, appearing to seem frightened, but I didn't know, my thinking wasn't clear right now.

"Ghost," Dom and Menace said as they were coming toward me.

"Take Kelina with y'all. I gotta find Tommie," I said, pushing her toward them.

"Tommie is with Jasmine, outside in the car. Come on. We don't have time for this. The police will be swarming this place soon," Menace said just as I heard sirens rapidly approaching.

"Don't worry. We caught one," Dom said. All three of us walked briskly toward the back entrance where a set of black trucks were waiting for us.

"How you want to play this, son?"

I sat back in the seat with fire dancing in my eyes. A nigga never in their life had tried me how they did tonight.

"Ghost," Dom said to me, but still, I remained silently looking forward as I slid into a dark place. If niggas wanted this side of me to reemerge, then let's go.

I'd been on some chill shit, but that was dead. Tommie and my fucking child could have gotten hit tonight.

"Take me by my condo," I said, addressing the driver. "Have them bring dude to the spot," I said to Dom.

"Old man, go home and see about your wife."

"You're mad, but don't get beside your fucking self. My name still rings bells in these streets. I was shutting shit down while you were in diapers, running around, pissing on your balls and shit," he hissed. "My baby girls were both in that place. It's up with me."

The truck grew silent as we all became lost in our thoughts. Once we pulled up to the condo, I told Kelina to get out and go inside the house.

"But—"

"Go!" I barked. Turning, she walked briskly toward the entrance.

"It's something off about that girl," Menace said.

"Same thing I've been saying," Dom said.

"Swing me by Jasmine's house," I told the driver, ignoring both of them. I had already peeped shit out tonight, but that was the least of my concerns right now. I didn't even give the truck time to come to a complete stop before I jumped out and damn near ran up the driveway and knocked on the door. As soon as Tommie answered the door holding her stomach, I started looking her over.

"Landon, I'm okay," she said. Lately, I had been Ghost every time she texted me, cursing me out, so I was happy to be Landon again. She was the only one I allowed to call me that.

"I thought something had happened to you," I said, pulling back from her to gaze into her eyes.

"Are you hurt? Did people push you too hard? Is my baby okay?" I asked, firing off a ton of questions then immediately pulling her into my arms again, hugging her tightly, not even allowing her to answer.

"I can't breathe," she said. Releasing her, my eyes grew a little misty as I thought about what I would have done had she caught one of those bullets. I would die if anything happened to her or my child. Whoever the fuck violated me like this had to fucking feel me because I was gon' paint the city red until I caught each and every one of them niggas.

"I'm okay, I promise," she said to me again, reassuring me.

"I love you, ma. I love you so fucking much. A nigga almost lost his mind back there."

"I was a little shaken up, but I'm fine," she reassured me. "Is she okay?" Tommie asked genuinely.

"Huh?"

"Your girlfriend?"

"She's not my girlfriend," I felt the need to say.

"It's okay if she is. I was only asking was she alright because she seemed upset. That was a scary thing that we just witnessed. I can accept the fact I lost you, and I'm coming to terms with that because it's all my fault. No need to be bitter. I'm at a place of acceptance now," she was saying until I silenced her long ass speech with a kiss. At that point, nothing else mattered in the world to me.

CHAPTER 10

AMBER

"So your ass really sent them boys to run down on him at his grand opening?" Chelsea asked as we sat around my living room, passing a blunt back and forth. She had proven to be a good friend to me and stuck by my side when damn near everybody else turned their backs on me like I was the only one in the wrong. Even my momma was looking upside my head, talking about, how could you do Tommie like that?

Shit they need to be asking Rodney's ass that question and be mad at him. So this nigga didn't get any blame? Yeah, Tommie was my best friend, but damn, sometimes you couldn't help whom you loved. I was already in too deep when this nigga up and told me she was his girlfriend, and we couldn't be together anymore, like my feelings didn't matter.

I made the decision that I didn't want to give him up, so I called him over one night, got his ass sloppy drunk, popped a million holes into the condom, and fucked him better than anyone had ever fucked him before. Yeah, I was young and dumb and believed a baby would make him stay, especially since I was giving him a Jr.

Shit, I got a tough dose of reality when that nigga still played me to the left. We continued to mess around here and there, but he never wifed me. Even when I sent him all that shit about Tommie and made dude walk over to her that day she came over. That was why I didn't open the door—so he could have time to shoot his shot. Shit, I told his ass to hug her and give her a kiss, but you know niggas could never follow directions properly. The pictures I had were enough, or so I thought.

Yeah, he beat her ass, but his ass still didn't move me in and put me on the pedestal I rightfully deserved. I wasn't a damn side chick when I was there before, during, and after her. It wasn't my fault I fell in love with a nigga who continuously promised me the world but only gave me his ass to kiss time after time again. The heart wanted what the heart wanted.

"Hell yeah, I had niggas shoot his shit up. Fuck he thought this was? Nigga, I ain't forgot. Ole bitch ass nigga. His mammy should have taught him not to put his hands on females. I'm not Tommie or them other hoes him and his cousin be hitting on. I'm a bitch that will rock with yo' ass. I hope them jack boys didn't miss either," I said, accepting the blunt she passed back to me as I took a long pull from it.

Shit had got my blood pressure up just thinking about it. I bet they thought I had let the shit ride, but hell naw. I was sitting back in the cut, waiting for the perfect time. Just when I was like *fuck it, I'll charge that shit to the game*, low and behold, Jasmine's black, ugly ass posted on Instagram about a grand opening Ghost and Dom were having. I knew them niggas wouldn't be expecting the shit, so that was when the plan was formed.

Speaking of Ghost, he may have been a bitch ass nigga, but he was fine as hell, and the fact his money was longer than a football field made him that much finer. But all that went out the window when his ass put his hands on me. The real question that I was trying to figure out was, how this bitch Tommie got two niggas to wife her up, and how she didn't know they were related? Hell, Ghost grew up in the A. Him and Dominic sexy asses were from Bankhead.

They only recently moved away like maybe six or seven years ago. Well, before she got with Rodney, Tommie was a real nerd and kept her nose in a book, so that was probably how she never crossed paths with him. If I could go back to her eighteenth birthday, I would have never forced her to go to that concert with me instead of studying for a test. Here I was, tryna be hot in the ass and get the attention of the cute ass up-and-coming drug dealer who I was secretly fucking and, instead, managed to direct his attention to little miss Tommie instead.

"Girl, you're funny, but you're right about that. Better hope that nigga don't find out, though," she said, nervously laughing, but I saw right through that shit. Scary ass. "Bitch, bye. I'm not fucking worried."

"I heard he was nothing to play with. I'm just saying he did punch your ass down once. I would hate to see what he would do if he found out you had them run in and shoot his shit up."

"Shit, fuck Ghost and his gang of bitches. He not gon' find out, because them niggas not no snitches unless you telling, and snitches get stitches," I said, mugging her. I would hate to have them niggas get at my only friend, but if she tried to turn snitch, it was lights out for her ass. I could talk all the shit that I wanted, but if Ghost ever found out it was I was behind all this, I was skipping town. Fuck all that.

"When you going to get Karter? It's been like what? Two months."

"Shit, his daddy wants to keep him, and I'm fine with that. I love my baby, but hell, if I could have given him back after I found out that Rodney still wouldn't make me his woman, I would have because that's the only reason I had him. He is a handful, and I'm with him all day, every day, listening to him talk me damn near to death with his bad ass," I said, smiling.

I may have been trifling, but I did honestly love my son, but shit, he was with his daddy and not a stranger, and it was his turn to do his part anyway. If he suddenly wanted this Daddy of the Year award, I wasn't gon' stand in his way. Shit, I was enjoying this freedom. Of course, I still called and gave Rodney's ass a hard time, putting on this role like I wanted my baby back, and he'd better not have him around Kelly, but shit, that was all a front.

She actually thought I was mad when I saw her posting my baby on her Facebook with new clothes and shit she'd bought him. I might comment, being petty and threatening to beat her ass, but again, that was just a front. Baby, spend your money, bitch. My baby surely will rock all that shit, sis. Gone get him the new Foams and Jordans; he'll be the freshest four-year-old at daycare. When he goes to pre-k, they'll be welcome to buy all his school clothes as well. Like, I wasn't sure in what world baby's daddy's girlfriends really thought the baby's mommas be hard down mad they were doing for our child. Baby, I was petty and did shit to fuck with people, but I wasn't really mad like that.

"Let's go to Citi Trends to find something to wear tonight," she said, standing up and putting the bud out.

"Bitch, what I look like wearing something from Citi Trends around some get money niggas?" I asked her. She must have bumped her head or some shit.

"See, that's your problem. Everything doesn't have to be designer. Citi Trends' clothes be cute as hell. It's not what you wear; it's how you wear it."

"Uh huh, that's all fine and all, but bitch, my ass won't be caught dead in that shit. We can hit the mall."

"Fine, I'll go to Citi Trends once I drop you back off," she said, and I agreed with her because that was her best bet.

Later on, I was just getting out the shower when I walked inside my bedroom and damn near jumped out of my skin as I stared at my on-again, off-again boyfriend, Kenneth. I know, I gave Rodney's ass a hard time, and this whole time, I had a boyfriend—well, not the entire time because I had just met Kenneth about a year and a half ago.

"Damn, baby, you scared me," I said, walking over to where he was and sitting in his lap. As you could clearly tell, we were currently back on, and I was excited he was finally back in town. It had been about five months since I'd seen him. "How was your business trip, baby?"

"It was fine. What you been up to while I've been gone?" he asked.

"Nothing but missing you all day, every day."

"Is that right?" he asked me, stroking his bearded goatee.

"Yeah," I said, not making eye contact with him.

He just stared at me for a minute, and I was afraid that he didn't believe me or, worse, had heard about all the drama that happened to me. Technically, it wasn't my fault, because when Tommie and I reconnected, the hoe never told me she was fucking Ghost. Had she informed me, I would have politely put her on game about that being Rodney's cousin. So really, if you looked at it, it was that bitch's fault.

"Baby, I need you to do me a favor. Do you think you can do that?" he asked suddenly, smiling as he pulled me down to his mouth and hungrily attacked it.

"What you need, baby?" I asked, breaking away from the kiss.

"Well," he said.

"Tell me. I promise I'll do it," I said, knowing that I would.

"I need you to tell me everything you know about your son's father Rodney's organization and his business relations to Ghost."

CHAPTER 11

TOMMIE

"How are you really, Tommie?" my momma asked as we sat in her room, watching TV. I tried to come visit her at least once a week or as much as I could. Since I found out about the cancer, she'd had three surgeries, and they tried to aggressively attack the cancer with chemo, which didn't seem to be working. She seemed to only get sicker and sicker to the point where she voluntarily stopped altogether. She still took her medicine, but she refused anymore surgeries and chemo and insisted if it were God's will, then she wouldn't fight it any further.

Being pregnant and already having a lot on my plate, I tried not to think about it that much because it would drive me crazy. Especially being that I felt as if I wasted so much time staying in the house, depressed in my own situation, that I ignored my family. If only I would have been stronger and not let Rodney control me, I would have noticed her condition earlier.

"Stop doing that, baby," my mother said like she was reading my mind or something.

"I can't help it, Mommy," I said, feeling a little girl all over again.

"Child, don't worry about me. I'm okay, baby," she said with a smile on her face. I didn't understand how she could smile through the pain, because I knew she was still in a great deal of it, but she said acceptance brought her happiness and peace.

Giving up the argument, I said, "I'm okay, Momma. I saw Landon a couple days ago, and he has a girlfriend. I honestly wasn't as affected by it as I thought. I mean, I was hurt, but for the first time, I put him first instead of me and my feelings and emotions."

"Are you happy with that decision?"

"I mean, I just want to live in peace. I've come to the conclusion I would rather have some of him than none of him. It killed me day in and day out when his texts were not directed toward me nor inquiring about me. I realize now the major role I played in all of this. It's crazy it took a shooting for us both to realize we wanted to be in each other's lives."

"A shooting?"

"Long story."

"Seems like I have nothing but time."

"I was there, and still, I'm unsure of all the details, but I have a feeling Landon will get to the bottom of it, and it won't be pretty for the person responsible."

"Good. That sounds like somebody needs their ass handed to them. I know my Landon gon' handle that."

"Your Landon?" I asked her.

"Yes, I like him more than Rodney's trifling ass, and Landon comes to visit me quite a bit," she said, revealing something to me that I had no idea about.

"When did this start, and what do you guys discuss?"

"Don't worry about me and my son's business," she said, snapping her fingers at me.

"Oh, well excuse me," I said with a smile. It really warmed my heart at how well they took to one another, especially considering my mom didn't like anybody. Well, correction. She didn't like Rodney's ass nor any of his friends, which she had every right to.

"I'm so proud of you, baby. That's very big of you, and I love you so much. I know I may not have shown it in the past, but just know I was always your number one cheerleader, even if I was cheering from a distance. I know you think I was disappointed in you, but I just didn't agree with your decisions. That's all. However, you've tackled everything life has thrown at you and came out still standing. All I've ever wanted was what's best for you because you are so very young and gifted and still have your entire life ahead of you. Speaking of age, what are your plans for your birthday?" she asked me, catching me off guard because I seriously had forgotten all about my birthday in a few days.

With everything that had been going on, combined with me being as big as a house, I really wasn't excited about my birthday at all and possibly wouldn't do anything. I had no friends other than my sister and no real family here. The only gift I wanted was for Royalty to make her grand entrance.

"Probably nothing, Momma. I haven't even thought about it," I said.

I stayed with her for a few more hours before I left to head home. Making the long car ride back home, I was exhausted and more than ready to get in my bed.

There must have been an accident on the highway because the driver and I were currently stuck in this slowly moving traffic, going on what felt like an hour now.

“Can you turn the air up?” I asked, sweating profusely.

“Yes, ma’am,” Jimmy, the driver, said.

“Is it some way to get out of this traffic?” I asked him, getting antsy. My baby wasn’t in a good mood, for some reason, and was starting to give me a hard time.

“Royalty, don’t hurt Mommy,” I said, rubbing my stomach in a circular motion as I tried to calm the sharp pains that I was experiencing. Royalty was acting up tonight, and I knew I said I wanted her to come for my birthday, but I think I lied because I was feeling a pain in my lower stomach that felt as if someone were repeatedly cutting me. Just when I felt as if I were going to scream, it went away as if nothing had previously happened. Thankful for the peace, I laid my head back on seat, breathing heavily and wiping sweat off my forehead. I was sweating so hard at this point that my hair and clothes were beginning to stick to me. Letting down the window, even though it was freezing outside, I welcomed the cold air that rushed rapidly.

"It's cold as hell outside. You need to let that window up before you get sick. I got the air on high as it can go," he said.

"Well, it's not blowing hard enough for me. I feel like I'm about to pass out," I said, still trying to steady my breathing to the best of my ability. I was overreacting for no reason, and I must've just been overwhelmed from seeing my mother, which may have been why I was feeling like this.

Just as I had gotten myself calm, another sharp pain hit me that was so unbearable that I could barely breathe as it ripped up my side and shot down my back.

"Oh my fucking God!" I screamed.

"What the hell? You okay?" Jimmy asked as he turned around to look at me. Noticing that I had laid back and was holding my stomach, he swerved into the left lane and drove straight across the gravel that separated the highways and shot back the opposite direction, which had less traffic.

"Fuck, fuck, fuck!" I screamed as, one by one, I felt like I was being murdered by Freddy Krueger, Jason, and Michael Myers all at the same damn time.

"Hold on, man. Don't do this to me. Fuck! I was supposed to be off today; now look at me. A nigga don't know what the fuck he doing, bruh," Jimmy said more to himself than to me as he drove doing damn near a one hundred on the highway. "Fuck! Where the hell is a hospital?"

I went to speak to him to tell him to just GPS one when I almost passed out from the contraction that hit me.

"Royalty, wait, baby. Just wait, please," I said, crying hysterically. "God, help me!" I cried.

"What do I do, Tommie? Tell me what I do!" Jimmy said. "Shit, Ghost. Yeah, Ghost," he said, fumbling with his phone as he pushed the truck down the highway. Feeling my eyes getting heavier and weaker, I said a silent prayer to God to protect my baby as I closed my eyes and rested.

CHAPTER 12

GHOST

"That's all I could pull up, which should be enough. Give me a few more days to get the exact name of the confidential informants. That's not my department, and these cases are sealed tighter than a virgin, so it will take a while, but I will get it back to you," Matthew said as he handed me a few files. He was the captain of the police force's son and an up-and-coming FBI agent, who happened to have a gambling problem. He also had a financial problem that involved a wife, a baby momma, and a girlfriend, as well as a foreclosure on his home. It seemed his father had been supporting him and was all too eager to have the load lifted off of his shoulders—that, and the fact I'd deposited one hundred grand to his bank account for any information he could give. I was expecting a few names, but what I wasn't expecting was a whole FBI agent. *Bingo.*

"Appreciate this information. I expect to hear back from you very soon because this is a situation I needed taken care of like a while ago," I said, getting out of his car and walking back to mine, and I got in and tossed the file on the front seat, starting my car up and speeding off.

I felt like Kelina was either stalling me with information, or our having sex had considerably distracted her and interfered with her ability to do her job. Either way, I didn't have time for the shit, because I had a kid that would be here any minute, and I didn't need this shit, and like I said, computer hackers, trackers, and information was easy to come by for the right price.

Heading back to the ducked-off warehouse I used to use a lot in Jersey but had long since stopped, I pulled in, cutting the engine as I grabbed the file and got out the car. Walking inside, I shot the men there a head nod as I walked to my office, closing the door behind myself. Opening the folder, there was names and addresses of every officer and agent worker on the case, as well as all the supposed evidence they had, which really was a whole bunch of nothing aside from a sworn statement and testimony of an informant.

The men I had on Henry's mom weren't reporting anything out of the ordinary back either. Shit, I'd gotten more information in five minutes than Kelina had given me this entire time aside from the initial report she gave me. As good as she was at what she did, I knew she could have easily obtained all of this shit. Combining that with how distant she's been acting lately was enough to confirm that we definitely needed to focus strictly on the business aspect of our relationship—if we even still needed to do business together. With an FBI agent on my payroll, what did I really need with a tracker when the nigga could easily get me what I needed? Shit, I was beginning to not trust her anyway. The sooner he could get me those names, the better. Feeling victorious, I closed the file as I put it into a cabinet and turned a key, locking it securely back into place. Standing up, I walked out the office just as Dom was coming down the hallway.

"Nigga, where you been?"

"Helping Jackie find a house so she can raise up out my shit. We didn't find shit today, though."

"Bruh, you still got that broad there?"

"Man, only because of her daughter. Shit, I don't know what's going on in these streets, and bullets ain't got no name on them."

"Okay, you got that," I said as I stopped in front of a door, putting in an access code and walking down the stairs the minute the doors slid open.

Once we got to the bottom of the stairs, we were met with another door, which again required an access code. Once we were granted access, we walked into the room where I currently was holding one of the niggas we'd caught who shot up our grand opening.

"This nigga stank," I said, taking note of the fact he had peed and shit himself.

"A grown ass man who can't even go to the bathroom: a damn shame," Dom said, walking over to the table, taking a seat.

Pulling a chair up the bed dude was currently strapped to, I said, "So are we in a talking mood today?" Because to prove he wasn't a snitch, the nigga had held out on information for a while because he was under the misguided assumption I would just shoot him and get it over with. He was only on this bed because I had a doctor patching him up every day and even giving him blood so that he wouldn't die to prolong the pain.

Sparking a blunt up, I stood up from the chair and walked over to a metal box I had delivered today especially for him. I told niggas they didn't want this side of me to come back out, but they kept testing me until I snapped. Picking the box up, the contents of it immediately started rattling around.

"Nigga, the fuck you got in that shit?" Dom asked.

"This is for our friend."

"Let's get this over with so I can get stitched up by the doc and go back to sleep. I need my beauty rest," dude said. Laughing at him, I unclasped the box and turned it upside down, shaking the contents all over his body. I watched closely and a bit fascinated as the huge wild rats who had been captured and starved damn near to death, immediately started running over his body, attacking it.

"Damn, nigga, them some big ass rats, yo," Dom said, jumping back and grabbing his gun.

"What the fuck, man, ayy!" dude yelled. It was funny how that gangsta got turned down pretty quickly.

"I wonder how long it will take to bite through your flesh or, better yet, for them to eat a leg or something? You know you can still get patched up even if a few body parts are missing. Money can buy you the best doctors in the country, my friend."

"Okay, I'll talk, I'll talk! Just get these fucking things off me! You're one sick bastard!" he yelled.

"Talk first."

"Man, I don't know much. My homeboy asked me to do this shit with him and threw me some bread. I forgot the chick's name who sent them to get at you, but she lives in Atlanta," he said, moving his head from side to side, trying to keep the rats away from his face because his hands were tied to the bed.

"A bitch is behind this?" Dom asked. "Like on some 'thin line between love and hate' type shit?"

"That's all I know. Her dude the one paid everybody, and they really wanted us to get at Ghost."

"Shit, the only nigga you beefing with in the A is that nigga Rodney. I told yo' ass he can't be trusted. What I tell you? I said *that's a snake ass nigga*," Dom said, going on and on. My phone started ringing as I looked down and noticed one of Tommie's drivers calling me. Quickly answering the phone, he told me he had been calling me, and Tommie was in labor.

"Send me the address," I said, hanging up.

"Tommie went into labor. Shit, it's time. It's early as fuck, but we have to go," I said as my palms suddenly began to sweat.

"Fuck, bruh, take these damn things off me! I told you what you wanted to hear," dude said.

"Shit, that's good. Therefore, I have no use for your ass no more," I said, walking out the door and quickly running up the stairs with Dom hot on my heels. Once I got back in the front area, I stopped briefly to tell them to get the clean-up crew to get that nigga and those rats out my shit.

"You nervous?" Dom asked as we pulled into the hospital.

"Hell yeah," I truthfully said. Walking into the hospital, I got Tommie's information from the front desk and headed to up her room.

"Shit, you're about to be a daddy. I seen folks on the Discovery Channel passing out at the sight of childbirth," he said.

"I'm a real nigga. I got this," I said, but it didn't sound confident nor convincing. Taking a deep breath, I walked into the room to see Jas sitting in a chair, the driver, Jimmy, in the corner, and Tommie sitting up in bed with an IV in her arm, looking very much still pregnant.

"Glad I didn't miss anything," I said, walking inside.

"Where you been?" Jasmine asked, immediately going in on me.

"I've been taking care of business, but I'm here now, and I'm sorry. How much longer did they say you had to go?" I asked Tommie as I walked over to her bed.

Just then, the door opened, and a doctor walked in.

"Good evening. You must be the expecting daddy," he said to me.

"Yeah," I replied as I began rubbing Tommie's stomach.

"How much longer until she is ready to push and stuff, doctor?"

"It's hard to tell because she is not dilated at all. She's been here for about three hours, and we will more than likely keep her overnight for observations and send her home tomorrow. What she experienced was what we refer to as a false labor or, more commonly called, Braxton Hicks. They mimic labor contractions and symptoms, making you believe that you are in labor.

They are unexpected, and come and go so randomly it's hard to predict when they will start and stop. She was brought in unconscious and dehydrated," he said.

"Dehydrated?"

"Yes, her body isn't getting enough liquids. Tommie not having her breathing under control and hyperventilating is what caused her to pass out. She is to be on bedrest until this little girl gets here," he said, looking down at his chart. "Okay, I'll send a nurse back in here shortly." As he exited the room, I turned to Tommie,

"What I tell you about drinking water and not those cokes?"

"I do drink water—well, sometimes," she said.

"Jas, this is just as much your fault as well. You need to make sure she doesn't drink anything but water."

"I'm leaving tomorrow for another job, so I think she needs to stay with you until I get back," Jasmine said.

"You know she's not going for that," I said, smirking.

"She has a name, and she is in the room, very much awake," Tommie said. "I think it's a good idea so I won't be alone, but I don't want to cause problems with your situation."

"The only situation I have is the one I'm currently standing in."

"That sounded super corny," Dom said.

"Fuck you, nigga," I shot back.

"Good looking out, Jimmy," I told the driver.

"I was just doing my job," he said. Sitting around, laughing, and talking with everybody, I felt at peace in that moment.

CHAPTER 13

TOMMIE

"So what you want to do is practice your breathing because that's the most important step when going into labor and helps to ensure a successful healthy delivery," the Lamaze instructor said. I was currently in the living room of Landon's house, watching an instructor via YouTube and doing everything she said as I tried to regulate my breathing. I was nine months and officially tired of being pregnant. After I was released from the hospital, I came here and had been here ever since. I'd done everything possible to make myself go into labor, but nothing seemed to be working, and I was getting more frustrated by the minute. I asked them if they could just induce me and get it over with, and they told me that technically, my due date wasn't until

February 22, so if by March 8, Royalty still hadn't come, then they would induce me. Fuck March; she was coming by next week.

"Put one hand on your chest and the other over your abdomen. This is to ensure that you are doing the exercise properly," the instructor said, demonstrating how we were to breathe in and release it. While researching and reading up on false labors and Braxton Hicks, I stumbled across first-time mommies to do lists, and at the top of it was taking a Lamaze class because it walked you through controlling your breathing. Once I thought back to how I acted the day we'd gotten stuck in traffic, I knew this was exactly what I needed for when that happened. Deciding against booking a live course since I was technically supposed to be on bedrest, I figured this would do, watching it from the living room while I did everything they were doing as best as I could. Noticing everyone had a partner slightly put me in my feelings, but I was going to try not and let that bother me too much.

"Breathe in slowly while imagining your stomach is a balloon," she said.

Doing as I was told, I began to breathe in slowly, but when I released my breath, I passed gas as well—another thing I uncontrollably did a lot. Getting up, I wobbled to the bathroom, making sure that I didn't mess up my clothes or anything because until you had your baby, you had no control of your bowel movements or the number of times you urinated. Once I made sure I was good, I used the restroom, washed my hands, and returned to my place on the living room floor.

"What are you doing, bruh?" Ghost asked, scaring the shit out of me as he walked into the living room.

"Landon, you scared the hell out of me. I almost damn peed on myself," I said as I damn near jumped out of my body. With my hand over my chest, I said, "I'm practicing my breathing for when my real contractions hit. It's called a Lamaze class."

"Don't ever go back," he said.

Giving him a confused look, I replied, "Go back to what?"

"Calling me Ghost."

Looking down, blushing, I said, "We're temporarily calling a truce?"

"I can do that," he smiled.

Walking over to the Mac desktop, he looked at the huge screen for a few seconds before he kicked off his shoes and got on the mat with me.

"What are you doing?" I asked.

"Exactly what them niggas on the screen doing. Now hush and pay attention," he said, causing me to laugh at how serious he was. We were finally back in a good space, and I was liking every minute of it. For a second, I allowed myself to think that we could possibly be a family, but I quickly dismissed that thought. I didn't want him to be with me because of Royalty. I wanted him to want me because that was what he wanted to do. Whatever direction life took us, I was done fighting him, and if given a second chance, I would let him love me.

We mimicked the instructor as best we could with me really trying to be serious and him laughing and being his usual clown self. Everything felt so right, and I was overjoyed. After another half hour of doing that, I was tired, so we stopped. Getting up and going into my room, which used to be the guest room until I took over, I decided to take me a nap because I had really tired myself out doing that.

"You hungry?" Landon asked me, coming into the room where I was sitting on the bed, struggling to polish my toes. I had been meaning to get them done for a while now, and I didn't want to have to go into a real labor and have them looking like that.

“Yo’ ass has an inability to sit still, you know that?” he asked me, laughing as he walked over, taking the polish out of my hands. I stared at him confused as to what he was doing until he sat down and placed my feet in his lap.

“You don’t have to do that,” I told him, embarrassed he was seeing me feet look so bad.

“Woman, quit telling me what I don’t have to do. I’m aware of that. Now, I done see a Chinese lady do this, so it can’t be that hard,” he said as he began to polish my toes, concentrating hard as hell like it was rocket science. My heart melted as I grabbed my phone and took a quick picture for Snapchat, captioning it *my baby daddy better than yours.*

“How has your day been?” I asked him. I had started asking him that more and more after I realized how selfish I was being, only always thinking about my situation and problems, forgetting men were humans too, and no matter how tough they were, they got stressed and had problems as well.

“It was cool. I’m getting shit cleared up, so things are looking up.”

“You need help with stuff?” I asked.

“Help with what?”

"I mean, I put two and two together. I know you must be into drugs as well. I was with Rodney for years, so I know the signs. I'm just saying I could help you cook stuff if you needed."

"Let me stop you right there. Me and Rodney not even on the same level, so don't compare us. I don't need help; I pay for help. I don't sell drugs on the corner by the baggie; I move weight by truck loads. I don't answer to the plug; I am the plug. I'm the head nigga in charge," he said to me. "And you better not ever let me catch you calling yourself cooking any damn thing," he said, pinching the bridge of his nose. I knew he was mad, and that wasn't my intention to make him mad. I was only offering to help.

"I'm sorry. I just wanted to be of assistance if I could. I didn't mean to upset you, I just want us to go back to how we were, and I was trying to right a lot of wrongs I did the first go around," I whispered.

Dropping my feet, he picked me up as if I weighed five pounds and sat me on his lap sideways. Lifting my head up, he said. "I'm not mad that you asked me if I needed help. I love that you would risk it all for me, and you're really down for a nigga. I'm mad that nigga did some bitch ass shit by letting you cook that shit up. No real nigga would have his woman cooking that shit. I'm pissed off because while I've been searching for my queen, the whole time, this nigga had you, dogging you out."

Leaning forward, I threw caution to the wind and kissed him. What started as an innocent kiss quickly escalated into a full-blown make-out session as we hungrily attacked each other.

"You better stop this shit before you get this dick," he said breathlessly to me.

"That's exactly what I'm trying to get," I boldly said, looking at him with lust-filled eyes as I took it a step further by reaching down in between us and grabbing his dick through his basketball shorts and squeezing it.

"Don't play with me, ma, because I'm serious as hell right now. I'm two seconds away from fucking your world up. Shit, you be out of breath walking to the bathroom. Gon' on somewhere."

"The doctor said sex was perfectly fine unless I felt discomfort, so either put up or shut up because since I've met you, you've been talking shit about giving me something I have yet to receive. You might not be about that life," I told him. Hell, I think I was just saying any and everything I could at the point because I was horny as hell, and if I didn't get some soon, I was going to scream.

Without warning, this strong nigga grabbed a tight hold of my tights and literally ripped them until they tore. Then, he slightly lifted me so that he could completely tear the bottom half of the tights so that all I was left with were some ripped tights that had the ass out but legs still intact. Before I could protest, in one swift movement, he had his shorts down and had lifted me up and pushed himself inside of me.

"Oh my God!" I squealed as he filled me up completely. Some shit, you thought you were ready for until it happened, and then, you realized that maybe, just maybe, that wasn't what you wanted at all.

"God can't save you now," he told me as he lifted my shirt above my head and attacked my breast since I didn't have a bra on. My right nipple was like a hot spot for me, and as soon as his warm mouth latched on to it, my juices began to flow rapidly as I moved my hips back and forth on his dick.

"That's it, baby. Ride this muthafucka," he said, not moving as he allowed me to do my thing. I must have been moving too slow for him however because he grabbed my hips and started slamming into me repeatedly as he lifted me slightly off of his lap, allowing him a deeper penetration.

"Fuck, oh, wow! Oh! Ahhh!" I screamed as both pain and pleasure shot up my spine. I was loving and hating every minute of this.

"This what you wanted, huh?" he asked, fucking me from the bottom while I tried my best to fuck him from on top.

"Yes, this what I wanted, baby." I moaned out as I threw my head back. Snaking his hands down my legs, he eased them apart as he began to tease my clit, causing my legs to shake uncontrollably.

"This can't be what you want." He moaned as he grabbed a fistful of my hair, pulling my head back and attacking my neck but never easing up on his assault on my clit nor missing a beat fucking me into a coma. Every time I screamed, he covered my mouth with his and fucked me harder.

"You love daddy? Huh? Tell me you love daddy dick," he said with his hands still in my hair. That shit was turning me on so much that I felt like my entire body was on fire. He kept asking me the same question over again, expecting a response, but I could barely think straight to answer him. My vision was cloudy, and it felt like my hearing was temporarily gone. Shit, this nigga's dick was literally fucking my whole world up.

After I had an explosive orgasm and got myself together, he pulled out, lifted me up, and walked with me to the bed, laying me down as he began planting kisses all over my face until he landed at my mouth.

I hadn't had any penetration sex since I'd gotten pregnant, so after that organism, I was spent at this point and more than ready to curl up in a ball and suck my thumb. That was how good the shit was. Landon had a different idea as he passionately kissed me.

"We're not finished. What you thought this was?" he asked as he lifted one leg onto his shoulder, kissing up my leg and nibbling on it while hitting his dick against my happy place then pushing back into Heaven. "This shit feels so fucking good, bae," he said, moving his hips in a circle as he leaned over me, grabbing both my hands, placing them on either side of me and interlocking them within his. "I know you got four more of those in you, and I'm not catching mine until you get all four, so you better be well rested," he said to me as he pushed back inside me.

What have I gotten myself into?

About four hours later, we both lay spent inside his bed. Don't ask me how we managed to start in my room and end in his bed, because I was there and still didn't know. All I did know was I kept trying to tap out, but this nigga apparently didn't get tired. I wasn't sure what I was expecting the sex to be like, but that definitely wasn't it. True to his word, he refused to nut until I came four times. The last one was so stubborn. I almost died because my pussy literally felt as if I would fall off at any minute, but when he and that magical tongue slide down into my happy place, he literally sucked the fourth one right out of me.

"Baby?" he asked, kissing me on my forehead. Pretending to be sleep, I tried to lie very still because, shit, I couldn't even feel my legs at this point. I couldn't go again.

"Bae," he said again, this time shaking me. "Bruh, I know you're not sleep. You're funny as hell. Must think somebody tryna take ya lil' booty again. That was a lesson to you for all that shit you was talking. I told you this wasn't what you wanted," he said, getting out the bed and walking away. Coming back a few minutes later, he turned the lights on and came to my side of the bed as I opened my eyes.

"I just want to talk to you about something really quick," he said, looking a bit jittery. Sitting up, I propped myself up on the pillows and got comfortable. "I just want us to start over. I feel like we were on the road to building something beautiful until it was snatched away from us. I feel like we're both stubborn, and neither wanted to admit we really wanted to be with each other. It was easier to hate than love. Every day, I fight my feelings for you, and I'm tired of fighting and pretending that what we had was temporary or just for the sake of the baby. I love you regardless of my daughter. She's just an added bonus."

"If you allow me to, I'll do my best to erase that fuck nigga from your memories altogether because every day, you'll be too busy being treated like a queen to even remember how that nigga used to act," he said to me as I stared in his eyes, seeing all the love he had for me. The way he was looking at me had me floating on cloud nine, and I would be a fool to let this man go for a second time. I was in the process of answering him when I felt something cold sliding onto my fingers. Looking down, I got the shock of my life when I stared down at a rose gold, princess-cut diamond ring.

"I had this all planned out with a huge birthday dinner for you, but the doctor was adamant that you be on bedrest, so this will have to do. I ain't plan out a long speech or nothing; I just know my eyes were opened to a lot these last few days, and almost losing you was a wake-up call."

"But I'm fine," I said until he put his hands on my lips to silence me.

"Just let me get this out. When them shots rang out, all I could think about was you. I couldn't move past that thought. I want to wake up to you every morning and go to sleep with you every night. If I died tomorrow, I would die knowing that I got the chance to make you my wife."

I didn't know what to say as I looked from him down to the big ass rock that was damn near blinding me. I said I would give him another chance to love me if I were ever given the opportunity, but did that equal marriage? Were we rushing into this thing? My mind was filled with so many different thoughts, while my heart had only one answer.

"Yes," I said.

CHAPTER 14

DOM

“If you hear anything or think of something, give us a call,” the detective said to me. They had been coming by the shop every day since the shooting, but I always had the same answers for them. Surprisingly, we didn’t incur that much damage from the shooting, and it didn’t scare folks away. This was New York; they lived for shit like this. When news of the shooting flooded the streets that night, Fly Guys became an overnight hit. I couldn’t tell you what it was about shopping some place that had a shootout, but our first day open, sales hit five hundred grand. Pretty soon, I was going to have to hire more staff.

"Julius, I'm leaving for the day, but if anything serious comes up, please hit my line," I told my store manager.

"Okay, boss man. You know I got this, boo," he said.

"Aye, what I tell you about calling me that shit?" I grilled him. Yeah, he was gay, but the nigga came highly recommended, and his resume was pretty impressive. He had a vast number of social media followers, and he brought in a boat load of customers a day, so he was alright in my book.

"I'm sorry. It just rolls off my tongue," he said.

"Don't lose that tongue then," I shot back as I headed up to my office to grab my keys so that I could make it on time to my 2:00 p.m. appointment.

"This unit comes with central air and heat, as well as all electric appliances. The floors were recently remodeled, and the stove as well as the refrigerator are only a year old," the apartment manager said, showing us around the modest but cute apartment. "Down the hallway, the master bedroom has two closets, one being a walk-in closet the other a regular closet. There is also a half bath inside the room," he said.

I glanced over at Jackie to get her take on things because, apparently, nothing was good enough for today, being that this was the fourth apartment we'd seen since we started searching a week ago when I agreed to help her get a place. I had also promised baby girl I would help her mommy. That little girl was growing on me with each passing day but not enough to make me go Ghost and wife her junkie ass mother and claim her as my own. I liked to think of myself as Uncle Dom. That shit sounded better than Daddy to me.

"I like it, but it's small," Jackie said.

"I think it's the perfect size for you and your daughter," the manager said.

"Shit, it's a two bedroom. How many rooms you need?" I asked her, looking upside her head.

"I need more space," she said.

"Fuck that; she'll take it," I told the man, completely ignoring her simple ass because I was not looking at another apartment today. How the fuck you complain about something when you were just living in a small ass house with eight other people? She reminded me more and more with each passing day of all the things I didn't like about her ass, and this one was at the top of my list. Nothing was ever good enough for her. Shit, still,

I tried to give her the world, but I doubted she would have even accepted that shit now that I think about it.

"Great, I'll go get the paperwork ready," he said, scurrying off, happy to have made a sale.

"That's not fair, Dom. You said you would help—not dictate."

"Shit, I'm paying for this, so this is me helping."

"The rooms are too small," she said, itching. I hated that she scratched herself all the damn time. I guess because her body was reacting to not getting any of the usual drugs.

"You came to my house with a trash bag full of clothes to your name. What the fuck do you have to even put in this bitch?" I asked her because I really needed to know. Hell, she acted like she needed a thousand square feet or some shit. This place was 753 square feet with a full bathroom and a half bath. She didn't need shit else.

"You're going to be living here with us, Uncle Dom?" Jacinta asked me, looking up at me with those big blue eyes that she had.

"No, baby girl, but I'll be sure and come visit you all the time," I told her.

"Okay," she said, seeming to accept that answer. "Can we go to Chuck E. Cheese now?" her little ass asked. She didn't forget shit you told her because I had said that a few days ago, and she asked me daily about it. Deciding to give in, I said, "Yeah, lil' momma, we can do that."

"Yay!" she said excitedly as she jumped up and down, clapping her hands. It took us another hour to finish the paperwork and pay the security deposit and rent, but after we got the keys, we were on the way to Chuck E. Cheese to see that ugly ass rat with the big teeth and goofy ass outfit. They could have at least given the rat some swag and threw him some Js on because them fat ass Great Value shoes had to go.

Once we got to there, Jacinta grabbed Jackie's hand and started to drag her toward the games while I was left in charge of getting tokens and pizza. Walking to the counter, I was looking over what I wanted to get when I felt arms hug me from behind. I instantly got heated because everyone knew I wasn't big on being touched. Spinning around, I saw Morgan standing behind me.

"What you doing here, beautiful?" I asked her as I leaned forward and kissed her. I had run into her again after my store got shot up, and it turned out she's a cool ass chick.

“I brought my niece and nephew to give my sister a break. You know she just had the new baby.”

“Yeah, yeah, I remember you telling me that. Her husband’s still going to trial?”

“No, he was sentenced last week. Thirty years,” she said. Shit like that was what I wasn’t trying to allow to happen. If we didn’t get on top of this whole Fed case situation, we all could be looking at football numbers.

“Who are you here with?”

“I’m here with my ex and her baby.”

“Her baby?”

“Yeah, ma, that’s what I said. Her baby. The kid ain’t mine.”

“Just checking,” she said.

“So what if she was mine?” I asked because of how she said it.

“If she was yours, I would tell you to lose my number.”

“Shit, so you a diss a nigga because he got a kid?” I asked, looking at her suspect as fuck. Even though I had no kids and didn’t have plans to have any anytime soon, shit wasn’t sitting well with me that she said that.

“No, I wouldn’t diss you because you have kids. I would diss you because I don’t do deadbeats, and someone who would deny their kids, that's some little boy shit. Our first date, we discussed children, and you said you didn't have any. Then, you said your ex and her child, so if it would have turned out that, this entire time, it was your child, then that would have been a turn off that you were downplaying your child for me."

I didn't even think about it like that. Shit made perfect sense to me.

"I feel that. Whenever I do decide to have kids, nothing in this world would ever come before them.

"Uncle Dom, where are the tokens?" Jacinta asked, calling my name.

"Until then, I'm fine with being Uncle Dom."

Later on that night, I was upstairs, looking over files Ghost gave me from this FBI nigga when I heard my doorbell ring. I never had any visitors, so I immediately became alarmed. If it had been Ghost, his ass would have just used his key or called me. Grabbing my gun and making sure the safety was off, I slowly crept downstairs, trying to get to the door before Jackie's stupid ass opened it. Making it down the winding stairs and into the hallway, I saw that I was too late as I peeped Jackie standing there with the door open and Jacinta by her side.

"Who is it? I asked her.

"Umm," she said, turning to face me. Keeping my gun out and pointed toward the front, I grabbed them out the way as I stood face to face with the intruder.

"Why are you here? The fuck you want?" I asked Jasmine.

"I'm pregnant."

CHAPTER 15

GHOST

Don't mind you looking 'cause she mine, girl. She for me.

Fall off, she gon' hold it down, please believe.

Firearm, we roll around in the streets.

When I get home, it's going down in the sheets.

Don't mind you looking 'cause she's mine, girl. She a big, fine girl.

Every time she wind, she move her body like a spider.

And everybody watching all that ass she got behind her.

Money make her shine, but I don't mind 'cause I'm a grinder.

I was cruising down the streets, feeling good as fuck right now. I still had that lil' issue going on, but I had my girl back, and she was about to be my wife. Nothing else mattered. A nigga felt like I could conquer the world. The only thing that could bring me down was having to tell my aunt that I was killing her only child.

That shit was gon' break her, but Rodney violated when he had them niggas run up in our store, firing recklessly. That was sloppy work, even for that nigga. I wondered who the hell this bitch was who helped him pull this shit together. Kelly didn't look like the type, but at this point, I wasn't putting shit past anybody.

Kelina had been blowing my phone up since I dropped her off, and I was headed to the condo to kick her ass out. Shit, I still didn't know where she dipped off to when the shooting started, but I was gon' get to the bottom of everything sooner rather than later. Right now, I was officially off the market, and she would just have to deal with that.

Pulling up to the condo, I didn't see her car as I parked and hopped out. Putting the key in the door, I walked in and had to turn around and walk right back out. After I walked out and walked in again, shit still hadn't changed. The entire living room was filthy. There were empty food containers everywhere, empty bottles, half-eaten food, clothes thrown all around, and there was a foul odor coming from some area. The shit just smelled too bad to exactly pinpoint where. This place was filthy, disgusting and trifling.

How did I miss this shit? A nigga hadn't even been gone that long. Walking into the kitchen, there were dishes piled up in the sink, trash overflowing, and pots on the stove with old food in them. I left this condo about two weeks ago, and it was top of the line, and now, it looked like a damn dump. This had to be like a joke. I knew Ashton Kutcher's ass was about to pop out with some cameras, laughing and shit, talking about you've just got Punk'd.

Walking out the kitchen, I headed upstairs, scared of what I would see when I got there because her being dead would be the only explanation I would accept for this shit. Walking into my room, it was surprisingly clean. Grabbing a Gucci duffle bag, I started putting things into the bag that I cared to take, and the rest I would leave because I had no intentions of coming back over here for a while. Hearing her coming into the house, I kept packing stuff in the bag so that I could get the fuck out this slob. I would have a maid service tomorrow to get this place back together. I might even rent it out because I didn't see myself having any need for it anymore.

"Hey, baby!" she cheerfully said, walking into the room, carrying bags in her hand.

"So you gon' just pretend like you don't see that?" I asked her, looking at her in a completely different light.

"See what?" she asked, looking down at herself and around the room.

Pointing, I said, "That shit downstairs that looks like a garbage truck came and dumped everyone's trash out."

"You are over exaggerating. It is not that bad," she had the nerve to say. If I hadn't already had the pussy, I would have sworn it smelled just like this house. I didn't know how she could let the shit get that bad. I mean, in the past, when I came home, I would pick up things here and there, but it wasn't a lot. You never truly knew a person, I guess.

"Not that bad?"

"Okay, it's a little dirty, but I got busy and didn't have time to fully clean up. It's nothing; I'll do it today. Where have you been, and why have you been ignoring my phone calls?"

"Tommie went into labor. Well, it was a false labor, but after she left the hospital, I said she could stay with me since Jasmine had another hospital assignment to do, and I didn't want her there solo."

"Why you can't hire someone to be there with her?"

"I ain't about to have random niggas in my shit. That's my baby momma—my responsibility."

"Your responsibility, huh? This the same baby momma who I found out wasn't actually your baby momma at all but more so somebody's else's baby momma? Now, I've heard of men dating a woman with a child and growing so attached to the child that they still take care of it after they break up. However, that's not what you're doing, because this child's not even born yet. So help me to understand how you think this is okay."

"This nasty ass house done fried your brain because I know you surely have lost your damn mind," I told her, laughing. "Watch out, bruh," I said as I went over to the couch in my room to sit down so I could fold these clothes a different way so they could all fit into this luggage.

"I'm serious, Ghost. We don't need this in what we are trying to build. Now, I hope the rest of her pregnancy is smooth sailing, but I draw the line when it comes to her moving in with you until the baby is born," she said with her hands on her hips.

Grabbing my body, I squeezed myself extra tight just to make sure I wasn't dreaming and was actually awake. I went on to run my fingers through my hair that was currently in a curly mess all over my head opposed to the signature braids I usually wore. After I pinched myself enough to make sure a nigga was still there, I jumped up from my spot on the couch and had pushed her against the wall and grabbed her by her throat before I knew it. I wasn't actually choking her hard. I was applying just enough pressure to let her ass know I meant business. She had been gradually showing her true colors more, and I had to get this bitch the fuck away from me before they found her body floating in the river some damn where.

"Listen here, bitch. I don't recall asking you how you felt about shit, because your opinion doesn't fucking matter to me. If it came down to Tommie and my seed or your ass, there wouldn't be a damn choice to make, because you didn't even make the options list. I think it's best you stay fifty feet away from me at all times. As of this very minute, your services are no longer needed. You don't have to go home; the Hilton hotel is nice this time of year. But shit, yo' ass do have to get the fuck up out my shit," I said, releasing her quickly as she sucked in air, trying to catch her breath.

The crazy bitch started laughing. "So you really gon' move her into a place where we've fucked in every inch of? You must really love her if you're mad about me having a problem with you moving her in."

Saying fuck these clothes, I stuffed what I could inside and left the rest on the floor as I grabbed my keys and phone and walked out the room. She followed me downstairs, still yelling.

"I knew it, with your punk ass."

Making it to the living room, I was trying my best not to kill her ass as I tried to focus on making it to the door.

"So you not even gon' be man enough to admit the shit, huh? You love the bitch, and you're just using this as an excuse to go back to her. That's why it's a problem that I'm mad about it."

"Love her? Hell yeah, that's my heart, and pretty soon, she'll wear my last name. Mad? Hell naw. I'm not mad about shit I pay bills at, and I'd never move her into this small ass condo. She lays her head in my California king at my home," I said, wiping the smile off her face as I opened the door. "When I come back, be gone," I said, about to walk out, but I paused and stepped back into the door. "Never mind. On second thought, you can stay because I'm throwing the whole apartment away."

As I sped off, headed back home because I had been gone a while now and needed to check on Tommie, she started calling my phone.

"Bae, I'm on my way now."

"Can you stop and get me my favorite snacks?"

"I'm not getting that baby powder shit."

"No, chips and ice cream," she groaned.

"What's wrong?" I asked, becoming alarmed.

"Your child is being extra fussy today. She won't be still nor let up off my side."

"Daddy will be there soon to rub your stomach and put you to sleep," I said.

"That's probably why your child got an attitude now—all this extracurricular activity Daddy's been doing to Mommy."

Laughing, I said, "Daddy's baby better stop blocking. That's grounds for time out, but I'll see you soon," I said as I hung up, and I pulled up to Walmart. Getting out and walking in to grab Tommie some Ben and Jerry's ice cream and Doritos—the shit was like crack to her—my phone started ringing. Picking it up, I noticed it was Matthew calling me. Damn near breaking my finger to slide the phone to answer, I didn't give him time to respond.

"What you got for me?"

"I didn't get a name, but I got a time today that they would be meeting the informant."

"That's what the fuck I'm talking about. So you're sure that's the only solid evidence that they have that can indict us?"

"Yes, I'm one hundred percent positive. I'm sending the location to your phone now," he said before hanging up. Leaving the snacks—I would just stop and grab her something on my way back—I turned and walked back outside to my car.

Ding!

The information came through, and it threw me for a loop because it was in New York. They only knew me as Ghost in Jersey because I didn't move shit in New York, so that kind of paused me. Still, I was eager to know who the fuck this was. Calling Dom, he didn't answer as I drove to the location. Shit, the meeting was in an hour, and it was gon' take me forty-five minutes to arrive.

Pulling onto the street, I parallel parked on the other side of the street behind a car that gave me perfect view of the parking lot. I was simply going to wait until whoever this informant was showed up so I could finally know who it was and leave. Not having to wait long at all, I spotted a black Lincoln Town Car that I automatically knew was the Feds because that car screamed pigs.

"Okay, where's your snitch ass at?" I asked out loud. Half an hour later, when they didn't show, I was beginning to think this was either a dud, or they got scared and stood them up. I was getting ready to leave when I noticed a car creeping down the road. As it got closer to me and turned into the parking lot, I was able to get a better look at it as recognition set in because I knew that car all too well. There was only one person I knew that drove a custom-made, black Rolls Royce with personalized tags: my pops.

TO BE CONTINUED

34089738R00126

Made in the USA
Middletown, DE
23 January 2019